Injustice

A Kingpin Love Affair: Vol. 4

J.L. BECK

Copyright 2015 Josi Beck
Injustice, by Josi Beck

Cover design by Sprinkles on Top Studio LLC
Cover Photo by Shutterstock

Editing & Formatting by
Rogena Mitchell Jones Manuscript Service
Proofreading by AmiLynn Hadley

All rights reserved.

All rights reserved. No part of this book may be reproduced in any form or by any electronic or mechanical means- except in the case of brief quotations embodied in articles or reviews- without written permission of its publisher.

The characters and events portrayed in this book are fictitious. Any similarities to real persons, living or dead is purely coincidental and not intended by the author.

If you're reading this book without buying it, then that is stealing and that isn't okay. Please return this book to wherever you found it and buy your own copy.

Copyright 2015 by Josi Beck
All rights reserved.

Contents

ALSO BY J.L. BECK IX

COMING SOON XI

AUTHOR DISCLAIMER XIII

CHAPTER ONE 1

CHAPTER TWO 7

CHAPTER THREE 17

CHAPTER FOUR 25

CHAPTER FIVE 35

CHAPTER SIX 43

CHAPTER SEVEN 49

CHAPTER EIGHT 57

CHAPTER NINE 67

CHAPTER TEN 77

CHAPTER ELEVEN 85

CHAPTER TWELVE 99

CHAPTER THIRTEEN 105

CHAPTER FOURTEEN 113

CHAPTER FIFTEEN 119

CHAPTER SIXTEEN 125

CHAPTER SEVENTEEN...131

CHAPTER EIGHTEEN..139

CHAPTER NINETEEN...147

CHAPTER TWENTY..151

CHAPTER TWENTY-ONE...159

CHAPTER TWENTY-TWO...165

CHAPTER TWENTY-THREE...171

CHAPTER TWENTY-FOUR...177

CHAPTER TWENTY-FIVE...183

CHAPTER TWENTY-SIX...189

CHAPTER TWENTY-SEVEN...197

CHAPTER TWENTY-EIGHT..203

CHAPTER TWENTY-NINE..211

CHAPTER THIRTY...215

CHAPTER THIRTY-ONE..221

WORTH THE CHASE..233

ACKNOWLEDGEMENTS...239

ABOUT J.L. BECK...241

Also by J.L. Beck

—BITTERSWEET SERIES—

Bittersweet Revenge
Bittersweet Love
Bittersweet Hate
Bittersweet Symphony
Bittersweet Trust

—KINGPIN SERIES—

Indebted
Inevitable
Invincible
Injustice

A Kingpin Series - The Complete Collection including BONUS Novella – Infringe

—PROJECT SERIES—

Project: Killer

Coming Soon

Worth the Chase

Dangerous Desires

Bittersweet Reunion

Tainted by Her

Severed Ties

Project: Rouge (Project Series #2)

Author Disclaimer

This book is intended for readers 18+ only. It's a dark, erotic romance that contains copious amounts of violence, sex, murder, swearing, dubiousness, and other things that aren't suitable for a younger audience.

This book also contains graphic abuse, some that may trigger unwanted or hidden emotions. Please be advised that I DO NOT condone this type of behavior, and I DO NOT agree with emotional and/or physical abuse in any way, shape, or form.

This is a work of fiction, and nothing contained in it is based off my life or someone else's life. Please heed the warning when I say that this is dark. It's not rainbows and ponies; it's murder and darkness that blooms into love.

CHAPTER ONE

Isabella

THE FLOOR WAS cold beneath my hands, a blindfold covered my eyes never allowing a sliver of light to break through. I missed the sun and all the things that it brought like warmth, the heat that would coat my skin. I could hear someone next to me sobbing quietly. I had been just like her mere weeks ago. Now I was nothing but a shell of myself, betrayed by my own family and sold into a sex ring.

My hope was shattered, my thoughts of escaping this place disappearing the moment I realized I had nowhere else to go. This was my new home until I was bought, whether I liked it or not. I was beaten, battered and broken in every way, and the worse part was there was nothing I could do as I awaited my fate.

I knew what would come of me—nothing. I would be used for everything I could be, and then when the time came, they would discard me like yesterday's trash. I had been here months and had seen it happen time and time again. I had come to terms with the life I was being given.

"Tony says we need to move them the fuck out of here. Someone is coming." A man's voice I knew all too well echoed through the room, bouncing off the walls and flowing through my ears. I had no idea where we were, what was going on, or who it was that had me. I had been drugged, blindfolded, and forced to sit with my hands tied with rope behind my back when I was taken—or rather given away.

"All right, man." The other man sighed in frustration. "You take the left side of the room and I'll take the right side." A shudder worked its way through my body. I wasn't ready to be touched. I never would be. Maybe they would consider me crazy and just kill me outright. In the end, that would be better than what they would make me into—some drugged up whore.

"Let's go, Princess." One of the men growled in my ear just as there was a tug on my arm forcing me to stand. A scream threatened to break free of my lips as my muscles protested, and my body threatened to collapse to the floor. It was then my mind drifted. I was close to going into survival mode. Then again, wasn't that what I had been doing all along? When was the last time I had eaten something? Drank water? I could feel myself crawling back into my shell. *It only hurt if I allowed it to hurt.*

The hand on my arm tightened in warning. Pain was all I ever felt. "I said to fucking move." Rancid breath encompassed me, my senses going on high alert as I felt him right next to my ear. Forcing my wobbly legs to move, I followed behind him as he tugged me along. I could hear others moving around and wondered how many of us there truly was. Sometimes I even wondered if the other girls thought like I did, felt exactly as I did. *What were they going to do with us?*

"Now, you're going to go through this door and be a good little girl. No kicking, punching, screaming, or trying to escape. Do you understand me?" The anger in his voice promised horrible things and I knew if I tried to get away I wouldn't like what would happen to me. My teeth rattled as he pushed me, my foot catching on the door jam. With no hands to catch myself, I fell onto the cold dirt-covered ground. I could smell the earth beneath me and wondered what it would be like to become one with it. Fresh tears formed and slid down my face, yet I felt no emotion. Was there a way to shut it off? To make all the hurt go away?

"You klutzy bitch!" he whispered harshly, ripping me from the ground and pulling me back up to my feet, my legs still wobbly.

As soon as I could, I marched forward not wanting to draw more attention to myself. In the pit of my stomach my nerves unraveled. The desire to know where it was I was going and who I would be with was almost too much. As I stumbled further, the darkness covering my eyes still shielding me from my surroundings, I felt as if I were floating through time. Simply waiting for my moment to come.

"Over here, Princess." I tried to follow the sound of the voice but felt as if I were drifting further from it. Nervousness filled my veins. Anything could happen and I wouldn't know until the very last second.

"Two men coming in from the right stairwell." Another hushed voice muttered. The sound of guns being cocked filled the air. I felt like I was going to be sick, someone could die and that someone could be me. The other voices I could hear clearly before were now

INVINCIBLE

being drowned out by my own thoughts. *Was this some sick twisted game they used as a scare tactic? Was someone else going to come and take me? Had this been the plan all along?*

"Get over here, Princess." I could hear the aggravated anger in his voice as he ordered me to find him. I stood there frozen in time as I heard a door being kicked in. *Where had the man who pushed me through the door gone? Why wasn't he leading me to where I was supposed to go?*

"You cannot let them find her, Xavier." Another man spoke. I floundered around the room, backing up as much as I could in hopes I would bump into a wall—anything to give me some type of direction. Hushed voices surrounded me, and as I tried to pick up on what they were saying, I felt myself moving a million miles a minute as I continued to scurry around.

"Princess, get over here, or I'll be forced to put a bullet in your head." I stopped immediately, my steps wavering as I swiveled around in the darkness trying to figure out where they wanted me to go. The gag that had been placed in my mouth when they first tied my hands behind my back kept me from responding to their vulgar words. Saliva pooled in my mouth as I tried to swallow around the intrusion. Did I really want to scream out and tell them where I was?

The barrel of a gun was being loaded.

Sweat covered my body in a mist of sheen.

I was going to die.

"She's valuable goods, X." A muffled voice that sounded as if it were a million miles away met my ears.

"I got this, man. Boss will just have to deal with it." I had heard the bullet before I felt it. Pain seared through my body as a burning sensation radiated through my arm.

"You missed, fucker." A voice sounded in my mind, but nothing mattered but the pain. My body fell to the floor limply, my chest filled with oxygen, but I felt as if I was unable to release it. *This was it. This was my time. I had wanted this all along.* Blood dripped down my arm, falling to the cold ground with a thud. I was aware of everything that was taking place around me, but at the same time, I felt as if I were a spectator watching it all go down instead of the chess piece in the middle. My body ached and a pressure formed deep inside my head.

This is the end, isn't it?

"FBI. Come out with your hands up." *FBI?* I wanted to scream out, to tell them I was here, but I couldn't. Between the pain in my arm and the gag in my mouth, I couldn't form words if my life depended on it—which, at this very moment, it did.

Heavy boot covered feet crossed the floor, growing closer and closer toward me. I was on the verge of passing out, the smell of iron filling my nostrils. Inside, I was screaming... begging and pleading for someone to save me, but on the outside, I was as meek as a mouse.

"It's okay..." I heard someone whisper in my ear causing me to jump instantly. "It's okay. I'm here to save you." *Save me? Was this real or was I dreaming this all up?* I felt hands wrap around my head, they were large but gentle and offered something that I hadn't felt in years-comfort.

In an instant, the bag that kept me in darkness for months was being ripped away. The gag that contained every ounce of hate, anger and every admission I ever wanted to say was released from my mouth. Bright lights flooded my eyes. Black spots appeared

INVINCIBLE

everywhere as they tried to adjust. Instantly, my body felt shielded, protected, and warm.

I was being rescued. Someone was saving me from a life that had slowly taken everything from me. For the first time in months, I took a deep breath and didn't feel an ache in my chest. I didn't feel scared.

I was safe. I was being taken somewhere. I would be okay. I had to be.

Right?

CHAPTER TWO

Jared

PRESENT

I WASN'T SURE what bothered me more at this moment—the fact that my phone was ringing off the hook or that I had brought another chick home last night. *Fuck.* Regret filled every pore of my body. Every time I said I wouldn't do it, I did. There was no point in trying not to. I had already admitted to being a useless piece of shit who used women repeatedly as a way to cope with the person I had become. It was the easiest way to deal with the pain.

Hesitantly, I gazed down at my phone on the nightstand. *Shit!* A red explanation point showed back at me, under it showed eight missed calls. Six from Zerro and two from my sister, Bree. This couldn't be good. I ran a hand through my dark hair in frustration. I didn't want to do this whole family reunion thing again. I loved them, but I couldn't handle looking at their happily ever afters while I had nothing. It always felt like their happiness was suffocating me, drowning me without them even realizing it.

My nightstand started to vibrate again, and I pushed the red key sending it to voicemail. I knew I would have to answer it sooner or later. They didn't give up easily and knew how to play the game. There was no saying no to either of them. I was learning their moves though. I knew if they got to ten calls, they would stop. Either that or they would come over here. That's how it always worked. They wanted to save me from the personal path of destruction I was on when they knew there was no saving someone as lost as me.

"Time to go," I mumbled to the blonde-haired woman lying in bed next to me. She was gorgeous, I would give her that, and her body was tight in all the right places, but none of it mattered. She wasn't what I wanted, rather a temporary fix that allowed me to ignore my inner demons. *What was her name anyway? Joanna, Jessica, Jenn?*

She murmured a complaint, but I ignored it. If she wasn't out of here in ten minutes, then I would remove her myself. I had no reason to get up and move around right now, and truthfully, I didn't want to, but if it meant getting her out of here faster, then so be it. This alone only lead me back to my original thought: *What the fuck was I doing?*

Pushing her soft body off me, I got up and grabbed the pair of pants that had been ripped from my body the night before and thrown onto the floor in a haze. I pulled them on without a second thought. I knew better than to head out into the kitchen without clothes on. I had done that one too many times now. I knew what was coming and I would be prepared.

"You know, I expected a lot fucking more from you." I shifted around, a small smile pulling at my lips. I would love to say that I was surprised by his reaction, but I wasn't. This wasn't the first time he had come over because I wasn't answering the phone. To me, there wasn't an important enough reason in the world for me to be answering phone calls. I wanted peace and I wanted quiet, not to be hounded by my family. I didn't need to know what good they saw in me when all that mattered was what I saw in the mirror every day.

"Expecting something from someone is never a good thing, especially from someone like me who will only leave you disappointed. The only thing I can offer up is failure. Is that what you're seeking?" I retort as I situated my cup under the Keurig.

I could feel the tension between the two of us growing, "The whole pity party thing is getting super old. It's even worse when you know you have a family that loves and cares about you unconditionally, and yet you continue to live your life this way. And for what reason?"

Didn't he know I asked myself that same question every day? Eventually, I got to a point where I had to accept the person I was and the shit God had granted me in life. I owned it as my own. This wasn't a fucking pity party.

"I have no logical answer for you." I smirked, pretending like I didn't give a shit. It had been three years since everything went down. I had been glad, grateful even, for Bree becoming a member of this family, but I knew it would leave a gaping hole in my chest. Bottom line—my dad had found the one thing that made his heart whole again and I still hadn't.

Zerro's laughter filled the room. "You usually have

INVINCIBLE

an answer for everything, so I'll just pretend I never heard you say that." I turned around and leaned against the counter waiting for my coffee to brew. My eyes caught on Zerro. It had been a couple months since I had last seen him. He was almost always gone—off on missions left and right, bullshit here and there. We never knew where he was or what his jobs entailed and it had aged him. He looked older, more mature. His beard had grown out and his build was more muscular. He could probably kick my ass in flag football now. Did I care? Fuck no. I'd still give him a run for his money.

I gripped the edge of the counter, forcing myself to stay put, to not pour my heart out to my best friend. Men didn't do that. We kept that shit bottled up real tight, plus heart to hearts weren't my thing.

"Pretend all you want, Zerro. We both know I'm the best at it." There was no hiding the hurt from showing. I could see the flash of recognition in his eyes. There was something about him that was different but still the same. Regardless, he still saw me as the person I used to be. The one I so desperately wanted to be again. He saw everything but mostly the pain, every little glimpse I allowed to escape.

"Cut the shit, Jared. We all know something is up with you. The family needs you now more than ever." He paused and I could practically see his chest filling with happiness. "Bree, is having another baby." His eyes flickered with joy. I knew how much he loved her and my niece. Hell, I loved them, too. I just didn't have that—but I wanted it, and that, more than anything else hurt the most.

"I know everyone does. I'll make a better effort." I lied. I wouldn't. There was no way I was going to force myself into that situation. I watched the glee in his eyes turn to anger. He knew me better than I knew myself.

"No, you won't. You said that last time and the time before that, and for the last three years. No one knows what's going on with you." He tried to sound sincere, but there was no way I was going to have this conversation with him right now.

"Save the mushy shit for someone who cares," I growled as I turned to get some creamer from the fridge and the sugar from the cabinet. Once I had them both, I poured them in and began stirring.

"Jared, where did I leave my pant—" Janice, or maybe it was June——her voice cut off. Hell, I couldn't remember her fucking name for the life of me. I turned gazing over my shoulder just in time to catch the angry stare that only Zerro could give me. He didn't have to say he didn't approve… it was written all over his face.

"No idea, sweetheart. I do assume you can show yourself out, though?" I placed the cup against my lips, some of the liquid sloshing over the rim. The hot coffee burned my skin, and for a very brief amount of time, it allowed me to feel something even if that feeling was nothing but pain.

She stood there unmoving, her tits all but popping out of her dress. "Really? After everything that happened last night?" she questioned, her hands on her hips. I could feel the anger radiating off her in waves as she opened her pretty little mouth. A mouth that had served a way better purpose than what she was currently using it for. Why did I have to go for the blondes? They were the hardest to get to leave the next morning.

"This isn't like a new thing, sweetheart. The doors over there." I pointed to the front door ignoring the daggers that were being shot at me.

INVINCIBLE

"You're an asshole. You know that, right?" She shot over her shoulder before grabbing her pumps and heading toward the door. There was a smartass retort that was begging to be let free, but I held it in as I waited to hear the slamming of the front door. That was my signal to move on and let go of the words that were never said.

"You know it's really shitty of you to be like that." Zerro butted in. I rolled my eyes. Of course, he would — as if he were the most gentle of men back in the day. Instead of letting it go, I turned it around on him. The king of mafia had done far worse than I ever would.

"If I do recall, you did worse things..." I raised an eyebrow in questioning. His face fell and his eyes down casted. I didn't mean to be a dick, but for him to tell me I was an asshole when he had done the same thing not all that long ago was a complete contradiction. He was throwing stones at me for doing the same thing he had once done.

"I realize that now, but that doesn't mean you should go about—" I placed my hand up to stop him. I had no need to be lectured, let alone questioned. My motives and choices were mine alone, and I could live with that. I *was* living with that.

"I don't need a lecture, Zerro. I'm a grown man, and at the end of the day, I can handle the decisions I've made." I paused. He was ready to chew my ass out again. "What did you come over here for?" I asked changing the subject exceptionally fast. What I decided to do with women and my life was none of his concern. My hand clenched the cup tighter as I waited for him to speak.

I lifted my eyes to meet his only to realize he was growing angrier as the seconds passed. With his eyes narrowed at me, and his fists clenched, one would think he was ready to fight. I didn't want to do such a thing, but if I had to, to prove a point... my point, then I would. Just like that, the anger was gone replaced with a softness. One that said he understood.

"I need a favor." The second the words came tumbling out, coffee spewed from my mouth. Laughter on my part echoed through the house as I sat my cup down and got a napkin from the counter to wipe away the coffee on my face. This was rich coming from him. Especially after all he had just thrown in my face.

"You what?" I asked astounded.

"I need a favor, asshole. As in I need you to do something for me." I could hear his teeth grinding together. Alzerro King hated being indebted to anyone. If he had to pay back a favor, he would make sure he did it in blood. That's just how he was—well, how he used to be. Now he actually had to ask for help if he wanted it.

"That's weird. I'm pretty sure you just said you need a favor, and it looks like I'm chuck full out of em." I was being a dick, pouring salt into a wound I knew very well was already bleeding.

His fists released, and with them, so did the rest of the tension in his body. "I need your help. I have a woman who needs somewhere to stay. It's only temporary, for a couple months... maybe tops, but I don't have anyone else who can watch her nor that I trust with her."

My mouth hit the counter top. I was lucky I wasn't holding my coffee cup any longer because, had I been, I would've busted it to pieces. I couldn't form a word yet, but in my mind, all I was saying was *Oh, fuck no!*

"Did you just not see the blonde leaving my

house?" I stopped mid sentence, flabbergasted that he would even consider asking me. "Women and I don't click unless it's for one thing and one thing only." I reached for my cup but was halted as Zerro's hand shot out shoving the cup away. Coffee sloshed over the sides and down onto the countertop.

Fucker.

"I don't care about that shit. I care about this girl being kept safe, and I care about giving you something worth caring for. She's your responsibility. She's been hurt, Jared. For fuck's sake, man. Hurt in ways that I couldn't even imagine. I have done some bad shit, but finding those women in that basement made me cringe."

I wanted to slam the cup down and watch the glass shards fly. I didn't want him giving me anything to care about. There was nothing for me to care about but myself, and I wasn't even doing that properly. Instead, I sat it down on the edge of the counter, anxiety forming in my belly. The mere thought of caring for another human being pushed me over the edge.

"I can't do it, Zerro. You know it, I know it. It's not worth it." Zerro smiled and shook his head at me as if in disbelief.

"No, you think you can't do it. You can and you will. Just tell me, what if she was your sister? What if it were Bree? Better yet, what if it were Gia? You're telling me you'd turn your back on my wife and daughter? Your fucking blood, huh? I think not." His words hit me directly in the chest like a punch to my soul and my heart ached.

Moments seemed to pass as we both questioned our next choice of words. "She's relying on you and so am I. You need to take care of her. Make her comfortable and talk to her. Be the man we all know you can be. I'll be in touch." He turned away from me, walking away, and I hadn't even agreed to anything yet.

"You're leaving, just like that?" I was a bit amused with myself. Just minutes ago, I didn't want anyone here, but now—now, I felt like a part of me wanted to reach out to him.

"Yeah, someone has to go get the fragile cargo. See you in forty-eight hours, asshole." He pulled out a pair of black aviators and slipped them on as he started to walk away.

"Congratulations, man... On the baby. Tell Bree for me." My words had stopped him before he made it out the front door. He looked over his shoulder, lips drawn in sternly.

"I would if you actually meant them, but thanks. Next time though, actually sound like you're happy for us." I wanted to say something—sorry, thanks, anything really, but stopped short of letting the words out as I watched him walk out the door.

Anger surged through me, and before I could think of my next move, the cup in my hand was flung across the room, the contents splattering as the glass shattered against the wall

How could he? He knew how to cut me deep with his words, how to make me feel like shit when I was already feeling lower than the dirt beneath his feet. But most of all, he knew how I felt about caring for someone else. Caring left me open and vulnerable, and I just couldn't be either one of those things.

I watched the coffee drip down the wall and onto the floor. A brown puddle formed on the tiles in my kitchen. I closed my eyes, breathing deeply as I pictured

INVINCIBLE

the shards of porcelain flying in every direction when the cup cracked from the force of the throw. It reminded me of life. How it was always right on the edge of breaking.

Would there be any saving me from this?

CHAPTER THREE

Isabella

"MOMMA!!!" I SCREAMED for her, but it was useless. They were taking me, forcing me to leave.

"You must go, Isabella. It is for the greater good of our family." My mother insisted, trying to soothe me, trying to make me see the good in what they were making me do. Instead, a scream resonated through me louder than ever before. Tears fell from my eyes, each one a vivid reminder of the pain to come.

"Momma, don't let them take me... please, don't let them take me!" I was begging, praying for her to see I needed her, to see the wrong in all of this, to see that I didn't really have to go.

"Shhhh, child. You must go. This is for your family. Don't you want to do what is right for your family?" She scolded me like a child, her tone angry. How could she be angry at me for not wanting to leave? I didn't want to disappoint her, but I knew if they took me I would die, or worse yet, I would be used, broken, and

INVINCIBLE

thrown to the side like garbage once this was all over.

"Is it a deal or not?" the large man at the edge of the table demanded. He was an evil man. I could see the hate and suffering I would endure just from looking into his eyes.

"It is," my mother said, her words finalizing my death. She didn't even bother to give me a backward glance. Another scream erupted from my mouth and echoed through the room. My throat grew more coarse with each scream as I dug my fingernails into the flesh of my palms.

"You can't do this. Don't let them take me, Momma! Don't let them, please..." I begged. My mother's face stayed trained on the floor, unmoving and uncaring. Anger made its way to me. How could she?

"How could you do this? How could you do this to me?!" I demanded.

The large man who had made the deal with my family got up, scraping his chair across the floor loudly. I continued to bellow. My cries filled the room, completely uncaring of who he was or who any of these people was. None of it mattered to me. I was good as dead anyway.

"If you listen, Isabella, they will not hurt you. A deal is a deal..." The man tried to soothe me with his voice, but it just caused my stomach to roll. He smelt of sweat and smoke. I didn't want to go. *I wouldn't.*

"They will hurt me. You're lying to me. You're nothing but a liar!!" I screamed at him. Tears continued to fall from my eyes. I didn't care if it portrayed me as weak in the eyes of those who were going to break me down and kill me. All I cared about was in this defining moment of my life, I had the power to show my emotions. I had the chance to express myself one last time.

He looked at something behind me and then gestured to one of his men. For a brief second, I looked back and then I frantically turned back around, letting the knowledge set in that my life now rested in the hands of these evil men.

"If you don't defy us, then we keep our word. You defy us and we kill you. It's really quite simple. Understand?" His words were laced with a heavy Russian accent and his eyes held no emotion. They were just two dark little orbs, void of any and all feeling. I narrowed my eyes, the desire to spit in his face, to jab my fingers into his eyes, ran rampant throughout me.

"Listen to them, Isabella. Be good and nothing bad will come to you," my mother confessed, her voice nothing but a whisper to my ears. I turned my attention from the man in front of me and back to her. I didn't need to say anything to her, nor did I need to ask if she felt sorry. The words were written all over her face. She wasn't.

"It's time to leave," the big man stated as he sunk his meaty hand into my arm, gripping me tightly as if he knew if I was given the chance to run, I would.

"You will regret this, Mother," I said between clenched teeth. She no longer cared about me or the future that I could offer our family. My fate had now been sealed.

"Isabella." My name being called pulled me from the lingering memories of a past life I wished I couldn't remember. That thought alone told me I was far from okay. On a scale of one to fucked up, I was double fucked. Most days I knew there was no helping me. Not after everything I had witnessed and been forced to experience.

INVINCIBLE

"Yes?" I lifted my head in questioning, my eyes landing on a large man. He had two guns strapped to his side, an FBI badge hanging from his neck and was taller than I by a good foot. His hair was dark, cropped up top and shorter on the sides. As I eyed him more closely, I realized he wasn't someone to be messed with. Or at least that was the aura he gave off as he walked around the room. Call it a sixth sense or whatever, but I knew when people were good or bad, and I could tell this man had once been bad. But most of all, if he needed to be again, then he easily could be. Regardless of the dangerous vibe I got from him, he was one of the most handsome men I had ever seen.

"I'm Special Agent King. I wanted to come and see for myself that you were okay." His voice was calm, his honey eyes warm which, in turn, caused warmth to fill my bones. He watched me harmlessly yet intensely, wondering what the hell was wrong with me, I was sure. I had been fooled more than once thinking the people who could protect me always would. They didn't when push came to shove and to me, this situation wasn't any different. *Never again, I told myself.*

"I'm good..." I fidgeted with my hands, pulling on my sleeves to cover up the rope burn on my wrists. My skin was broken, bruised, and raw from where they had tied my hands too tightly. I wanted to make them disappear, to hide them so no one on the outside looking in would ever know I had been a victim.

What I had told him wasn't a lie. In fact, it was the truth—I was okay. *Finally.* It had been months since I had last taken a shower or consumed a meal every day. They believed throwing freezing cold water on us was just as good as actually allowing us to wash ourselves. The only times we were allowed to clean ourselves properly was for meetings with potential buyers or when we were being used for personal pleasure for the men who guarded us. Yet I had been rescued less than forty-eight hours ago and had showered more than once and was offered food on numerous occasions already.

I had taken three showers, back to back, feeling as if one just wasn't good enough. It was as if I could still feel the sweat that clung to my body and the dirt underneath my nails. It all disgusted me and somehow, still made me feel like a captive. Those feelings caused my stomach to roll with nausea as I shook my head, trying to shake the thoughts.

After being freed, I was put into an ambulance as they checked my vitals, rushing me to the nearest hospital. Three doctors came in and out of the hospital room they had put me in. The first two checked my mental state and conducted a full body exam to make sure I hadn't suffered any internal injuries. The last doctor to see me was a gynecologist. She was nice and tried to reassure me everything would be okay. She performed what they called a rape kit on me, making sure I hadn't been violated in any way. That was how I spent my first twenty-four hours free, being evaluated and having tests ran on me. Once everything came back good, the very next morning, I was released back under the FBI's protection.

"Hey..." The agent kneeled down onto the tips of his toes in front of me. His face was youthful with a bit of ruggedness, his eyes holding a concern for me I hadn't seen since I was a young child. Still, I could feel the edge, the slight darkness that surrounded him.

"I'm fine, really..." I reassured him with a small smile that felt completely foreign to my face. My lips were pulled tight against my teeth. It probably looked like I was making some funny expression due to the fact that my cheeks didn't know how to adjust to the movement. There was no gentleness in it. It was completely forced, and I'm sure it looked more like a grimace or worse.

He smiled back at me, his far more genuine than mine. "You don't have to lie to me. I'm not going to hurt you if you tell me you are, in fact, not okay. No one here is going to hurt you."

I knew that. I wasn't as broken as most of the girls they had found in that building. I had had been luckier than any of the others.

"I don't think you're going to hurt me." I brushed some loose strands of my jet black hair behind my ear.

Agent King watched me carefully before coming back up to his full height. "Things are going to be a little crazy in the next couple of days. We're going to be transporting you to a secure location where you will be safe. Everything you need and anything you want will be provided. There will be plenty of food and you can shower however often you want. You should know that your location is to be kept a secret, and you're not to contact anyone, including your family at any point in time. Doing so could result in them discovering your location and putting you and my men back in danger. Do you understand?"

Everything he was saying to me made complete sense, not that I would have a reason to call my family. They were the reason I was in this situation, why I was to be sold to the highest bidder.

"I understand." I didn't really feel like talking, even if it was safe to do so. I was used to being inside of my head. Talking lead to things being said that didn't necessarily need to be said.

"Do you truthfully? Because, honestly, you're taking this better than most would." He scratched the back of his head in curiosity as if he were attempting to figure me out. What he didn't realize was there was nothing to figure out.

"I had it better than most of the others. They had made a deal with my family." That was all I wanted to say about it. They may not have tried to engage in sex with me due to being promised to another, but it didn't mean they didn't make me touch them, and it definitely didn't stop them from groping me.

He nodded his head as if he understood. "All right. Well, then, you should be able to move back into this a little better than the others who were rescued. I do want you to talk to the person you're going to be staying with. Talking helps. If you let too much of the things that happened to you stay in your mind, it will eat you alive. I know I don't look like I would know, but truthfully, I do."

Something in the way he said it made me want to reach out and touch his words. Dive into them and find out what his story was, but like I said, talking was pointless to me. The things I would speak of would just bring misery and pain. I didn't need any more of that in my life.

"Everyone has their own struggles. If I want to talk about my time in hell, then I will." I built myself on being strong, on bottling up the pain. I wouldn't be vulnerable to anyone.

"Whatever you say. I will be back in two hours to transport you to the safe house. Prepare yourself accordingly." And just like that, he was dismissing me to walk away. I was grateful in so many ways, but

INVINCIBLE

anxiety still found its way into the pit of my soul. *Who knew the type of person I would be handed over to?*

I threw myself back onto the small cot and relished in the soft material beneath my hands, the luxury of a bed—a pillow. I closed my eyes and absorbed the memories, forcing the bad to the back of my mind as I hoped for good ones to come.

Only in my dreams was I truly safe from the destruction called my life.

CHAPTER FOUR

Jared

AGENT KING WAS as good as fucking dead the next time I got my hands on him. My house had never been cleaner than it was today. Even the pantry was stocked with food, something I hadn't done in months. There was an array of food, a wide selection of things for her to choose from.

The spare bedroom was clean and tidy. The room smelt of linen and crisp air. Gone were the old bed sheets from when Bree and Alzerro had stayed here, and in their place were new ones. I smiled to myself. It was as if I was the newest edition of Martha Stewart only with a dick.

Now I was sitting on the couch nervous as ever, my palms coated in a sheen of sweat. It had been years since I had cleaned myself as thoroughly as I had today; scrubbed my nails, feet, and my back. Usually, I just took a shower, washing my hair and body and then calling it quits. But today, I shaved, put cologne on, and combed my hair. It wasn't that I didn't care for myself. It was more that I didn't give a shit what other people thought about me. With no one to impress, I had no other reason to look as I did today. According to Zerro, she deserved, at the very least, a man who looked somewhat put together. That and the fact he all but threatened me to have my shit together.

"Fuck," I said out loud to no one but myself. Minx, my all white cat with black paws, rubbed against my leg. I had gotten him at an abused animal shelter over a year ago. He was my one and only constant in life. What I saw in Minx was something I saw in myself and it instantly drew me to him. Without him, I would probably be completely off the rails. How strange it truly was that a cat could hold me to the ground, but nothing else could.

The minutes seemed to tick by causing the wait to seem longer, which was pure torture. The time it took for them to travel from wherever it was they were coming from to my home was like standing on pins and needles. I could tell myself all I wanted that I wasn't the least bit curious about what was going to happen, but we know that would be a lie.

I scratched behind Minx's ears and listened to his soft purr. Man, he had it made, didn't he? Then I wanted to laugh because I showed him more affection than I did others. I was all kinds of fucked up.

With nothing but silence surrounding me, I would know the moment they were here, so I bid my time. No sooner had the thought left my mind, I finally heard the sound of someone driving up on my property. As the car doors slammed, I wondered if I should get up and greet them at the door or just sit here casually as if I were uninterested. I didn't want to seem overly excited about human interaction, but I also didn't want to seem completely disconnected.

The doorbell sounded, and I plastered on the best smile I could manage while getting up from the couch to answer the door. Just as my hand wrapped around the door handle, I had a second thought to just go back into my bedroom and ignore everything. Pushing that feeling away, I pulled my shit together.

Not wanting to waste another second, I opened the door. My heart sank into my stomach just as my eyes caught hers. Her dark skin was a color between mocha and a natural tan. Her hair reminded me of the night sky without stars. Her eyes were a coffee colored brown that almost matched her skin color. My eyes glided over her lips, certainly not missing the plump pinkness they exuberated. Shit, I could already picture myself sliding in and out of her mouth. My balls ached and my cock rose to attention.

Get it in check, Jared.

Time seemed to stand still as I stood staring. Zerro cleared his throat, bringing me out of my thoughts. Taking a step back, I gestured for them to come in, not feeling comfortable speaking yet. How would my voice sound after thinking about my cock in her mouth?

No thank you.

"Isabella, this is Jared. He will be your guard for a while. He knows you're entered into the Witness Protection Program and knows to report any suspicious activity." The air left my chest in a rush. *Her name.* Sparks seemed to fly between us as tension filled my body. Her name was the same as my mother's name. I took a step back, wanting to put some distance between us, hoping maybe it would ease the ache that was starting to form in my chest. I could feel Zerro's eyes burning a hole through my back at my hasty retreat.

With my back to them, I greeted her. "Hello, Isabella. I hope you find this place to your liking." If Zerro wanted to glare at me, then he would have to do so at my back. I could sense Isabella's eyes on me, but I ignored them. I would have to do so often. She was a temptation I couldn't allow myself to ravage. Finally, I turned around making it into the living room before doing so. The second I did, Zerro seemed to unleash his fury, his eyes promising pain.

We stood in silence staring each other down.

"Are you guys okay?" Isabella asked innocently, looking between the two of us. Her words had a foreign accent to them, making me question how she knew English so well.

"We're fine," we both said in unison. Our stares became more heated.

"I'm just going to, um…" Her voice trailed off as she walked away to check out the house. Or at least that was what I hoped she was doing and not trying to make her escape.

"I know that look," Zerro mumbled just as she got out of earshot. I raised an eyebrow up at him while crossing my arms over my chest. My demeanor was defensive for a reason.

"Did I not tell you I eat pretty girls for breakfast? Or did you block that out of your mind?" I had warned him. I had told him all I was good for—he needed to learn to open his ears and stop trying to implant the good he saw in others into them. There was no room inside of me for Zerro's positive thoughts.

"Did I not tell you that I don't give a fuck?" He snarled stepping into my space. His chest was almost touching mine as fire filled my veins. *What the fuck?* He needed to pick a beef with someone else because my give a fuck was broken.

"I'm pretty sure you tell me you don't give a fuck all the time. Not much has changed there. I say I don't want to do something, you make me do it anyway..." I mocked him with a smug smile. I knew all the right buttons to push to send him over the edge. That's why, when his fist hit my face, I should've been expecting it. His knuckles slammed against my cheek causing me to stumble on my feet unsteadily. I fell to the ground a few steps back as I rubbed the side of my jaw, feeling the pain radiate downward into my chin.

Fucker.

"What the fuck was that for?" I blurted out, jumping from the floor. He could try and beat the responsible sense he wanted me to have into me, but it wouldn't do him any good.

"For being a fucking prick. You need to look at her like a life that needs protecting, not one of your blonde bimbos. I'm not even sure what the fuck is going on with you, but all I can say is to get your shit together and be prepared to fight for her. She's not just a *thing*. Her life, body, every part of who she is, belongs to the Russian Mafia. She's lost, used, and abused, and you need to take care of her." He leaned into me, and I swear to God, the look he was giving me was one I had seen many times when he was the King. "Or I'll take care of you. Understand?" He pressed harder against me until his chest was vibrating against my own in anger.

We were nose to nose, our anger on the verge of boiling over. I took a deep breath. I wasn't going to have a fucking fighting in my house. This was my sanctuary—that and I had just cleaned it.

INVINCIBLE

"If I wanted your advice, I would have asked for it. I might not be the best guy in the world, but as of right now, I'm the only one you have, the only one you trust. So if you want me to keep up my end of this deal, I suggest you take a step back and clear your head. If I need you, I will call you. Until then, get the fuck out of my house." I was pissed that he had come in here and threw his weight around as if he owned the place. I was doing him more than a favor by not handing him his ass.

He shook his head and looked at me sideways. "You're lucky you're Bree's brother and my best friend because, if you weren't, I would've laid you the fuck out by now. Get your head in the game." He acted like what he was saying actually meant something to me. I loved Bree and my father, even him in a brotherly way, but I had never felt so disconnected from them as I did right now.

"You're lucky I respect you and see you as brother..." I sneered wanting nothing more than to push back. I felt like a ticking time bomb waiting as if everyone was trying to push me until I blew.

"You're asking for a reason to fight. Something is eating away at you, and I have no idea what that thing is. All I know is it won't help you to fight others over your own internal struggle." His admission was a smack to the face and a slam to the chest. I tightened my fists forcing myself not to punch him or lash out with words. Even if I didn't want to admit it out loud, he was right. My problem had nothing to do with him or my family. It had everything to do with me.

"Leave. I don't need your philosophical analysis. " I gritted my teeth. The energy between us grew building and building. Seconds ticked by before he turned, raising his hands above his head as he headed back toward the door.

"I'll check in with you soon…" I watched as he left, a smug look crossing his face as he slammed the door behind him. I stood staring at the large wooden door, my eyes gliding over the wood. My fist itching to hit something, to feel pain even if it were only for a second. Silence surrounded me and a vein in my head started to bulge. How could I protect someone when I didn't even care if I lived or died?

Prying my eyes from the door, I contemplated what I should say or even do. The second I turned around, my eyes landed on hers. *How long had she been standing there?*

I stared into her eyes, the coldness in them sending a chill down my spine while the darkness in them called to something deeper within me. There was something inside of them. The way she held herself on the couch told me she knew fear—pain. It seemed she was broken into so many pieces and there was no way anyone could reach her. Darkness was her favorite, and we both were so very much fucked.

Two people full of darkness, hate, and hurt colliding was like a tornado waiting to destroy. And I would destroy. After all, I wasn't very good at keeping things in one piece, especially hearts.

"You don't have to look at me like a broken piece of glass. I won't cut you unless you get to close." A smile pulled at her lips, but it was tight.

Forced and fake.

For some unforeseen reason, it made me want to make her smile, not only that, but I wanted for it to be genuine. To see her teeth, her lips no longer hiding them. I wondered if mischief would twinkle in her eyes or if that small amount of light left in her would shine through?

"Well, I will. I'm not a good guy. I might not be like the people you were rescued from but believe me when I say I'm no better." I eyed her face for some type of reaction but got nothing. She was like a chalkboard washed cleaned. Nothing gave way to what she was feeling. She was void of all emotion. Just like me. *Fuck.*

"With that said, we need to lay down some ground rules. No leaving the house without me or without my permission. You're to stay indoors unless told otherwise. My house is your house. Use what you'd like, watch what you want, and eat whatever is here. But you're not allowed to make phone calls, and you're not allowed to ask questions. I make the rules. I don't want this to be a prison to you, but you're here to be protected until further notice," I said sternly, unblinking to the look in her eyes.

Her lips stayed slack, her hands fisted in her lap. Her hair was styled around her face with light curling at the bottom. I wondered if it was nearly as soft to the touch as it looked.

"Hmm, while this place will be just like home then." There was a hint of anger in her words, but I dismissed it. I had no time to listen to her melodramatic attitude. She wasn't worth the time or energy. My job was to protect her, and I would try with all my might to keep it just at that.

Protection. Keep telling yourself that.

A bubble of laughter formed in my throat.

Funny how my subconscious was a bigger asshole than I was.

"It will be better than where you came from, I can tell you that much. Stay out of my way and all will be good." Making myself move, I headed for my bedroom needing air away from her. I had never expected someone so dark, compelling, and tempting. I knew it would be a woman, but I didn't know she would be attractive or nearly as alluring as she was.

I walked into my room and straight out onto the patio, slamming the glass door with so much force, I worried it might break. The air seemed to be the only thing that could calm me down. I strained to get more oxygen in, forcing myself to take in a couple of deep breaths of fresh air.

Space and time—that's all I needed. I could do this. It would just take some time. I could push her away if she thought even for a second she could weasel her way inside of me. I would build the walls up around me as high as I possibly could.

That's all I needed. Space would save us both. It didn't help that every time I muttered her name, I would be reminded of the woman I lost. I would have to get over it. I had made it this far without her memory. I wouldn't allow it to haunt me now.

That woman in the other room had no clue the kind of chaos she was causing inside of me and she never would because I was locked up tighter than Fort Knox.

No one could penetrate my walls.

CHAPTER FIVE

Isabella

RULES.

THEY WEIGH THE heaviest on me. They are what keeps me trapped here. Never being allowed to go anywhere alone or to make any phone calls. Not that I would even want to do that. It's just knowing that if I wanted to, I could freely. The mere thought of being able to do so is nice.

The freedom of it all. Yet, I can't.

This place should be my sanctuary, a place where I feel safe, and in a way, it is. I don't think Jared would try to hurt me. I don't think he would ever lay a hand on a woman. I can tell in the way he carries himself. But the fact that these walls around me feel like a prison, as if I traded one cell for another makes me feel like I'm suffocating and there seems to be no chance at surfacing.

"I'm making dinner." Jared's deep voice wraps

around my thoughts, pulling me from my mind. I lift my eyes to meet his face but am greeted with air. He had already walked away before our eyes even had the chance to connect. A deeper coldness seems to shadow me as I start to feel more alone now than ever.

Today marked the third day of silence from him. He only talks when he has to, and even when he does, his sentences are short and straight to the point. It's obvious he doesn't want me here, nor does he want to be my guard.

My safe haven.

"Great," I mumble under my breath to myself. Insanity was on the verge of taking over. At least, when I was being kept as a hostage, I had something to feel. *Fear.* Here I feel nothing but silence. He's heavily guarded all the time in every way. Not giving me one chance at knowing who he is. He gives me no option, no chance of escaping the memories that cross my mind each day.

I can hear him in the kitchen, pots and pans being thrown around hastily. As he curses under his breath, it causes a spark of energy to form inside of me. Without hesitation, I cross the living room floor and come to a stop at the threshold of the kitchen as my eyes wander up and down his body.

I love the way his muscles move as he walks around with his back to me, his hand gripping the pan he just grabbed from the stove. I should be scared of men–of him, cowering somewhere in a corner in fear. I suppose in some ways I am scared, but something about Jared makes me feel free. *Safe even.* There is a compelling nature to him that causes me to be drawn in, like a magnet to their polar opposite.

I shake my head and try to remove myself from my

inner thoughts. He hates me. I could see it in his eyes and feel it in his words. My time in the trade showed me things like this, not only that, but it showed me things I never would have wanted to see in my life. It exploited me to very real pains, fears and hate that I never would've experienced had I continued to live a normal life.

"Why are you staring at me?" His voice was gruff, reminding me that I was in fact ogling him. Not just that, but I had been caught doing so. I casted my eyes to the ground and swallowed down the words I desperately wanted to say. When it came to my own emotions, talking did me no good. I needed to work through them on my own. However, it would've been easier to speak my mind openly if there was someone that wanted to hear what I had to say.

I knew that living inside my head was bad, and eventually, it would eat away at me if it wasn't already. I needed to talk to someone, to express myself, but Jared wasn't that person. He wouldn't be there for me when all the stones fell.

The room grew quiet except for the sizzle of chicken in the frying in the pan. When I finally got the courage to lift my head, our eyes met. In his eyes, I saw pain mirroring my own. Then, just like that, the invisible wall that separated us fell in place once again as he turned his attention back to the stove. For the remainder of the time, I stood there silently, afraid talking or asking questions would be overstepping some sort of unseen boundary.

He pulled out some plates and situated them on the counter, gesturing for me to make my own plate. My feet refused to move as I questioned the possibility that this could be a trap. It had been forever since I had been

INVINCIBLE

allowed to get my own food. I stared at Jared, trying to figure out what it was he was thinking as his facial expression reflected mine.

"Are you hungry?" he questioned. I nodded my head yes, causing a flurry of hair to shift forward. Why was I feeling shy like he could see right through me? At first, things felt casual, but now they felt heated—as if someone had taken a blowtorch to the two of us.

"Then get some food because I don't know if you know this or not, but in America, we men like to eat." His remark wasn't meant to be hateful or mean, but I couldn't help the jab that I felt to heart because of his words. I wasn't American. Technically, at least not fully. My father was an American on vacation in Russia when he met my mother who was a native of our country.

A tinge of pain formed in my chest. I missed my parents—my family. Even if it was their fault, I was in this situation. To me, the love you had for those who created you would never go away, the void of losing them would never be filled. No one could love you as unconditionally as a parent could. I liked to think my mother still loved me and that she realized the choice she made was wrong. I knew when she sold me, it was because our family needed the money. I had brothers and sisters who still needed to be taken care of. Being the oldest put the responsibility in my hands.

"Right." I stepped forward, unsteadily. I was a bundle of nerves, still unsure of how to handle all the open space and other options. I reached for the plate, gripping it like a lifeline as I placed some salad, chicken with white sauce, and noodles onto it. Grabbing my silverware, I headed for the table. There was a pitcher of water and two glasses sitting on it already. I poured myself one and then Jared one, setting his glass near the chair he had sat in the last three nights.

We both took our seats, cleaning our plates in a matter of minutes. A full belly was foreign to me as was getting my own portion of food. To me, it was a treasure that never seemed to last long enough.

"What was it like?" he asked out of the blue as I got up to place my plate in the sink.

"What was what like?" I countered turning around, my eyes meeting his.

He looked at me with a dumbfounded expression before answering. "When you were being held hostage, what was it like?" I gripped the counter wondering why he would even care to know, let alone ask. My body felt as if it was stripped bare. His eyes seemed to see deep inside my soul—to my fears and sadness.

"Why do you want to know?" I narrowed my eyes for the first time ever at him. I had a fire burning inside of me. No one asked questions like that. He got up, shoving himself away from the table and crossing the room with his glass of water in hand. His grip was tight matching the same tension in his jaw and I understood it, the feeling as if you were being pulled tight.

"Because looking at me as you were earlier is a good way to find yourself back in a situation you don't want to be in. I'm not a good man. I've told you that. Don't look at me as if you want something when your mind isn't even in the right place. I'm strong, but I'm not a saint. Remember that the next time you look at me." The brown in his eyes turned dark and his voice was nothing but complete rawness. He was attracted to me. He felt the same pull I did, but he didn't like it. His feelings, the desire to want something yet hate the very thing you wanted were feelings I too felt.

"I'll look at you however I want to look at you." I

piped in without thinking. My hand going up quickly, covering my mouth. I waited for him to lash out, to talk down to me, or to hit me. I had never spoken to a male in such a horrid manner before. My blood turned cold as I waited for him to react.

A small smile pulled at his lips as he placed his own glass in the sink. My heart rate picked up again, unsure of the motives behind his smile. "You're free to express your opinion, Izzy. Never think that I would harm you for it. Just know I saw the fear in your eyes after you spoke and nothing bad will come to you here."

Everything he was saying was giving me whiplash. He pushed me away and then told me it was okay to stand up for myself. He feared my touch and my closeness but loved my courage and my bravery. He was an enigma that I wouldn't ever be able to figure out.

Unable to muster up a word, I stepped away from him and headed into the living room thinking maybe if I put some distance between us things would cool down.

"I didn't mean to scare you." I heard his voice behind me and it caused me to stop right in my tracks. He was lying. He wanted me scared. It would be easier to push me away when all of this was over. I knew that better than anyone did. Hell, it was my one and only true vice when it came to others.

"Yes, you did." I shot back, still facing away from him. I could feel the air between us thicken. I wondered if he would walk behind me and wrap his arms around me. Worst of all, I wondered what it would feel like to be loved and cared for by him and to feel his heartbeat against my chest.

"No. I really didn't mean to scare you. I know you have been through a lot of shit, and I don't want you to—" His words cut off and a sigh filled the air. "It was a really big dick move to say that to you." Was he apologizing to me? He couldn't be.

Turning on my heels, I attempted to put some more distance between us not realizing how close he truly was. He must've crossed the room while I faced away from him. My eyes glided over his chest, arms, and shoulders before meeting his face.

"But you did, because just like me, you're afraid of allowing someone to get close to you. Everyone leaves in the end, right? So, while I accept your apology, I know you meant every word you said. Fear causes us to speak words we normally wouldn't." I was astounded and a bit shocked that I had spoken out in such a way, yet I understood his emotions as much as he did. He might be able to hide it from everyone else, but he couldn't hide it from me. His very emotions were something I dealt with daily.

His face fell, the shock showing in his eyes. He had to have known I could see right through his bullshit. Agent King did as well. There was no way he could assume he had fooled me.

"This was a mistake." He sneered, baring his teeth. Anger is the second thing to rear its ugly head right next to fear when you don't want to admit your faults when you feel trapped. Instead of calling him on it, I allowed him to think he had won and watched him turn his back to me. His footsteps were heavy with annoyance as he walked away from me.

I heard him mumbling under his breath but never stopped to focus on what it was he was saying. Instead, my eyes stayed trained on his body, watching every

INVINCIBLE

step he took away from me. Desperately wanting to reach out to him but knowing it would do no good, we were both two very different people on a crash course with reality. Our vices were the same.

When two people fighting the same battle collided, it would be like gasoline and a match waiting to be struck. It wouldn't take much to cover everything that made us who we were as we burned with fire.

CHAPTER SIX

Jared

MY THROAT FELT tight as I begged him to let me see her. Where was my momma? Why wasn't she home? Something inside of me said there was something wrong.

My dad hung up the phone, tears falling from his eyes. He never cried. He was strong. Why was he crying? Dads didn't cry.

"What's wrong? Where's momma?" I screamed, my voice filled with panic.

"She's gone, son." Three words that changed my life forever. Pain radiated through my body in a way that made me feel as if I was being ripped apart. I could feel a piece of me being pulled away. That piece being my momma.

I awoke covered in sweat, my hands gripping the sheets and my eyes squeezed closed as tight as I could make them. It wasn't real if you didn't see it with your own eyes. That's what I always told myself as a kid when the memories hit me full force.

It took three to four deep breaths before I released the sheets and popped an eye open.

My brain failed to catch up with my ears because, as I allowed the fear to slip away, a scream broke through the house. I waited a moment to see if it was merely my mind playing tricks on me or if it was Isabella.

When another scream filled the air, this one much louder than the previous, I felt compelled to get up from my bed, hardly realizing what I was doing. My feet stopped just short of her bedroom door. My stomach was in a knot. I didn't know if I should go in or not.

I went through the motions of feeling her pain, understanding, and knowing the nightmares wouldn't go away no matter what you did. It was up to you, the person going through them, if they would continue to plague you. My father always told me, *your dreams are your biggest fears played on the big screen in your mind.*

"No… please, no…" she cried out. Her voice was filled with so much sadness my heart seized, stopping in place for a brief moment. I pushed the door open a little bit, just enough for me to push in through the small opening. My eyes glided over her body, and I knew I had to do something.

She was laying on her side in the fetal position, one of her hands was clutching her chest, and the other was gripping the bed sheets as if they could hold her to this world. An ache formed with me and I found myself walking toward the side of her bed. Knowing that I would never be able to fall asleep with her fighting her biggest fears right down the hall from me.

My body caved, recognizing the pain she was

feeling as its own. I looked down at my flannel sleep pants and my naked chest knowing I would regret this in the morning. Lifting her just barely off the bed, I placed her softly against the pillows on the other side of the mattress. The bed was a queen, but looking at it now, somehow it seemed so much smaller with both of us in it.

"Fuck," I whispered. My body was telling me it was okay to be attracted to her. After all, she was a woman, and she did have a killer body, but it was more than that. I was drawn to her darkness. I craved it.

I slipped into bed next to her without another thought, knowing if I didn't move now, I never would. The sheets soft against my skin, my body began to calm.

In a moment's time, I was lying on my back facing the ceiling as she rolled over snuggling into the side of my body. I wanted to sigh into the air above. It was going to be an extremely long night. I was so wrong to think I could fight off her demons by being here, though.

I was about to become the biggest, meanest, realest monster of all of her demons. My fists clenched tightly, my teeth grinding together to keep me from reaching out and touching her. I didn't want this. I didn't want to feel drawn to someone. Especially her. She had more baggage than American Airlines. Yet I found comfort in her pain, knowing for once, I wasn't alone in the darkness anymore.

Slowly but surely, my body relaxed, allowing my breaths to come in slower and my mind to drift off to something I had never thought would come—sleep.

* * * * *

INVINCIBLE

WARMTH COVERED MY body in a blanket. A blanket that moved and was soft to the touch and had a nice pair of tits attached to it. My eyes popped open, panic seizing me as I tried to figure out where I was and why the fuck I wasn't in my own bed.

As I got my shit together and the panic washed away, I could hear Isabella's shallow breaths. The events of last night coming back to me, reminding me of how I comforted her. I wanted to curse myself, yet I had never felt so refreshed.

Her body moved against mine as if she wanted to embed herself into my skin. We were spooning, her back to my front. My cock was stiff and had found his own home right between her ass cheeks. I wanted to apologize or at least say something, but what was there to say? All I knew was it was much more than morning wood.

Her breaths stayed calm telling me she was still asleep, so I took that moment to take her n completely. To look at her the way I had caught her more than once looking at me. I watched the movement of her body as she took every breath, staring at her full lips that were parted, her dark skin reminding me of mocha. I was growing harder and harder by the second. What was wrong with me? This was so wrong, yet it had never felt so right.

I wanted to grip her hips, pulling her into my groin. Getting as close to her as I possibly could, but refrained knowing it was the wrong move to take without her permission. I shouldn't even be lying next to her, let alone wanting to grind my hardness against her softness. But I couldn't pull myself away from her, not even for a second.

She started to stir, her body moving just enough to

tell me that she was waking. Her luscious cheeks pushed harder against my cock, causing a low groan to fall from my lips. Her eyes popped open, the expression on her face was anything less than horror.

I was an asshole.

CHAPTER SEVEN

Isabella

I COULD FEEL him. Every single inch of his body was plastered against my own. Fear began to fill my veins. I had never allowed a man to be this close to me, so why was I doing so now?

I pulled away from his body, the warmth leaving me, the coldness returning as a tinge of sadness masked the fear. I had no reason to feel any emotions toward him, yet I did. I rolled off the side of the bed, pushing from it as fast as I could.

"It's okay, Izzy. I wasn't going to hurt you." He spoke softly, his voice hoarse with sleep. His face was brighter than normal, and he even had a sign of happiness in his eyes, but that didn't help to unthaw me. I was scared—more than that, I was afraid of what I was feeling inside of me. The dream I had last night was one I had many times before. It pushed me to the brink of destruction, centering on my first few nights in the *trade*. Tremors of fear racked my body throughout the night as I relived the terror in my dreams.

"It's not okay. You were…" My face started to grow red, embarrassment taking over.

Jared rolled his eyes and had I not been startled from the bed, maybe I would've laughed. "I wasn't doing anything. I heard you last night. You were screaming. I didn't know what to do, but something told me to check on you." I could hear the sincerity in his voice. Nothing on his face said he was lying, yet here I stood afraid to move. Afraid that if I did, I would be questioned about that single movement.

"I…" I stumbled over my words unable to get them out properly, my hands wringing together in front of me. We had gone from enemies to two people sharing the same bed overnight. It felt perfect and wrong all at the same time.

"You what? I wasn't going to do anything to you…" He paused, his voice bordering on angry. "I mean if you're worried about this…" He pointed to his penis and I about choked. I had touched one, even been told to suck on one, but I was afraid of it. Afraid of what it meant, of what it did, and what it would cause the other women who were in the trades with me.

"It was against my skin…" I paused briefly. "My butt." I was startled at the sound of my own voice. Had I spoken that out loud?

Recognition formed on Jared's face as if he understood what I was getting at, outrage and dejection seeping into his features.

"I would never, and I do mean never, force myself on you or any woman. Morning wood is something that is extremely common for men of all ages. It doesn't mean that we're attracted to you, and it doesn't give us the right to take what we want." He didn't look at me as if I was an object for his pleasure. Instead, he watched me most likely wondering if I would have a mental breakdown right this second.

What he didn't realize was his words calmed me. He cared, even if he said he didn't and even if I was afraid of what was forming between us I wanted to welcome it with open arms. I needed something good in my life. Something pure, something worth living for.

"So you weren't going to do anything?" I questioned just to make sure, encouraging myself to remember that Jared wasn't any of those men I had spent time with while in the trades.

I could tell he was upset by my question as he pushed from the bed. His body filled with aggression and tension. He stretched before me causing parts of my own body to react.

"Of course, I wasn't going to do anything. You were sleeping, for fuck's sake. I don't get off on taking advantage of women." He stepped into my space, forcing my back against the wall. Fear filled my belly, but so did something else. The feeling of being loved and wanted.

"If I wanted you, you would know it. And I most definitely wouldn't have to take you unwillingly," he said smugly, his eyes lingering on my lips. I was just about to say something when he took a step back and pushed past me to get out of the room. I stood there attempting to catch my labored breaths. Jared caused butterflies to form in my stomach, but he also caused me to feel the unknowingness of being with a man. The feeling was foreign but exhilarating all at the same time.

I waited until I heard the slam of his bedroom door before I closed the door to my room and settled back into my bed. The walls would have to be enough of a barrier for now. I held myself together, my arms wrapped tightly around my midsection. My mind drifted back in time to that dream when I thought the end was near. I needed something, anything to keep my thoughts off the present, even if it meant I had to head back toward my past.

Shifting into an upward position, I pulled my knees into my chest and pushed my hair over my shoulder so I could weave my fingers through it. I did this to stay calm. It had become a calming technique for me to keep my mind in the right place.

"Secure all the girls and place them on the right side of the room. I need to take photos of them to send to the buyers." I knew the voice like I knew what light against my skin felt like.

A meaty hand clamped onto my arm, pulling me to my dirt covered feet. My clothes were tattered and worn, my shoes and all possessions gone. I had nothing but my thoughts here and some of us didn't even have those.

The man's hand gripped me hard. His fingers dug into my dirty flesh until I knew there would be bruises. They always loved to rough us up and beat on us, making sure the injuries were far and few between and always out of sight.

No one would buy you if you were damaged. Being bought was your one and only chance at freedom. You'd be a fool not to want that.

"Her," someone said to my right as I was slammed into the unforgiving ground, my knees giving way. It had been days since I last had food or clean water to drink. They were depriving all of us of the things we needed simply because one girl refused to willingly give her body to one of the guards.

"Smile pretty for the camera, bitch." I could smell his rancid breath even through the bag that covered my face. They didn't just want pictures of our faces. They had already gotten those, now they were taking pictures of our bodies. A hand was placed firmly on my shoulder keeping me in line, forcing me to kneel straight. My knees dug deeper into the dirt, rocks embedding themselves in my skin causing pain to radiate throughout my body. Tears formed in my eyes, but I squeezed my lids shut, telling myself someday I would get out of here. I wouldn't allow myself to die here like the others before me.

"Move her and bring the next one in," someone new said as the hand on my shoulder eased up, moving the pain to another part of my body. The hand reached into my hair, gripping tightly as he pulled me to my feet. I forced the scream that desperately wanted to escape my lips, to stay deep inside of me.

Stay strong, Izzy, I told myself.

Allowing them to see your fear, allowed them to know they had some type of control over you. If they could scare you, they could do anything.

"I want her, boss," a man growled into my ear, his hand way too close to touching my breast. I imagined myself screaming, someone hearing my pleas and God granting me an end to this insanity.

"You may touch her above the clothes only." I wanted to beg, to tell him no but kept silent, cursing them in every way I could inside of my own mind.

Remember you have your thoughts. I repeated the words over and over again in my mind, thinking if I repeated them enough it would make it easier for me to believe. It would give me hope knowing they couldn't touch my thoughts.

INVINCIBLE

The man pawing at my breasts fondled them with both hands as I stood still, feeling disgusted in more than one way. Tears fell from my eyes, and I was thankful the bag was in place. I didn't want them to see my weakness. Didn't want them to know what they were doing really hurt me.

Minutes seemed to pass as agony took over.

One hand stayed against my breast while the other headed south. I could hear his heavy pants, his breaths against my skin.

"I will have you. This sweet, untouched pussy will be mine someday..." he whispered into my ear. My stomach revolted as acid threatened to spew from my throat. My insides curled as I tried not to recoil from his touch.

His fingers roughly rubbed against the material of my panties that covered my most intimate part. "Please stop..." I cried out softly, praying he would. Even if it were only for a second. I just wanted one person to show me they were still human and that all hope wasn't completely lost.

A harsh laughter filled the air. "You're begging me to stop now, but very, very soon, when you're mine, you will be begging me for more."

His hand that was against my breast moved to my chin gripping it tightly. My teeth ground together as my jaw clamped shut and fear coated my insides. I felt trapped, wanting to struggle against his hold, but at the same time, not wanting to give him a reason to knock me below his feet.

"Do you understand that this cunt will be mine? You're mine, Isabella." He hissed my name. Seconds passed with no interaction, all that could be heard was the furious beating of my heart and his heavy breaths against my cheek.

With a shove, he released me, and I fell to the hard ground. I had never been more relieved in my life to be shoved away, thrown away like yesterday's garbage. I didn't want any of the other girls to have to take punishment for my actions or my place for the things I refused to give to these people, but when it came down to surviving, I would do anything that I could.

I shuffled against the dirt floor and into a corner, unsure where exactly I was in the cell. I needed to find my way back to my cot. I was on the verge of collapsing on the floor when I heard the screams of one of the other girls.

Her cries were muffled as if she were far away. "Stop doing this to me. Stop hurting me," she pleaded. She didn't understand that pleading did her no good. They didn't care if they hurt us. Their job was to break us down into nothing, making us soulless individuals who would do anything they wanted. They didn't want women—they wanted puppets.

They wanted us weak, not just physically, but emotionally and mentally, as well. I continued to crawl on the floor until I came to the wall. My fingers digging into the ground beneath me, begging for a way out as if it would magically appear before me.

"You will learn this is how we do things here. Do you understand me? Nod your head yes if you do." The woman cried out in pain as the sound of a whip hitting flesh filled the air.

My heart ached, breaking in two knowing the pain she was enduring. They had been more than nice to me. I was dirty and felt upon, but I had never been a victim of their rage or felt the bite of the leather against my flesh.

INVINCIBLE

"You will speak only when spoken to. You will follow these rules or you will face the consequences." Another slap of the whip against her skin. Tears fell from my eyes for the pain she was receiving.

It was then I vowed to break free of this place, even if it got me killed.

CHAPTER EIGHT

Jared

I HATED MYSELF for leaving her there like that, even more for cornering her and making her feel like a trapped animal. I knew what she had gone through. I had been briefed on it by Zerro, but nothing made it more real than seeing the fear of what I could do to her reflected in her own eyes. I gripped at my hair, trying to find a reason for what I had done.

You're an idiot.

I wanted to laugh at myself, out loud like a crazy ass person just so others could see me for who I really was. I wasn't the good guy. I wasn't stable or happy. I had none of the things going for me that Zerro or Devon had. I was drowning helplessly in the deep end with no escape in sight.

You're not good enough for her.

My nails dug into my palms as I stared at myself in the mirror. I hated the person I had become but failed to do anything to fix it. I had allowed the simmering rage,

INVINCIBLE

agony, and hopelessness to carry me away from all those that I loved.

They don't love you, I told myself.

Comforting her was wrong, wanting her even worse, but now I felt starved as if she had been my first fresh bite of food in years. I didn't need to be pulling Isabella into my shitstorm called life. She had her own problems, problems that I would never be able to handle. She couldn't handle me. Today showed me just that, yet here I was trying to grasp at straws for something. Anything really to keep going to her, to keep her here. I splashed water on my face thinking that it would help wake me up from my asshole state, but it did nothing.

You're not her hero. You're her darkness. You will break her and hurt her more than she already is. Why can you not see that you're her destruction, her damnation, her downfall?

Staring in the mirror at the man who was not worthy of someone like Isabella, I made a vow to distance myself, to protect her when needed, but I would never allow myself to get close to her like that again. To feel her warmth against my coldness. To feel the softness of her curves against my hardness. Her shallow breaths would now only be a memory.

I slammed my fist on the countertop, forcing the words inside my head to stick. They had to—it would be the only thing saving her from me. From there I showered, dressed, and made my way out to the kitchen. The smell of freshly brewed coffee met my nostrils.

I rounded the corner, my eyes meeting hers immediately. The look in them were neutral but had an amused undertone. I felt a pang of guilt because I was about to become a bigger asshole than I had previously been, and I knew more than anything she didn't deserve to be treated this way.

"I made coffee." She sounded happy about such a small feat and I smiled in return, acting as if I was unaware of my actions.

"I see that. Thank you." My voice remained the same, the words slipping out as I prepared myself a cup. I needed to clear the air and to remind her that what had happened this morning wasn't going to ever happen again.

We all had to fight our own demons—even as tempting as it was to help one another through them.

"Thanks for—" She seemed to stop thinking about what it was she wanted to say next. "Being there for me last night even if I wasn't aware of it. I know you know some of what I went through, but sometimes, the nightmares get out of control…" She continued on, her voice soft and sweet. I clenched my fist gripping the coffee mug in my hand. I was so consumed with her, with the way her lips moved, and how her voice sounded, I failed to notice the coffee in my cup as it sloshed over the edge. I yelped out as the scolding hot coffee fell against my skin.

"Fuck," I cursed, running to the sink to run some cold water over the burnt flesh.

"Oh, my goodness. Are you okay?" She purred against me, her body rubbing against my side as she attempted to examine my hand. I hated what I was about to do but knew I needed to. After all, it was better this way.

"I'm fine," I said coldly, pulling myself from her grip, which in turn caused her to cower back a step. I could see the fear and hesitation in her eyes as she

INVINCIBLE

realized what I had said. I had just doused her pleasant mood with cold water. I had ruined her day with my shit behavior.

"I was just checking—" She looked slightly startled that she had said something.

"I know what you're doing," I growled, pulling away from the sink. I needed to get away from her, away from all of this. I was stifled, feeling buried underneath it all. The desperate need to confess my secrets to her was smothering me like a thick fog of smoke.

"Did I do something?" Her voice sounded somber as I allowed myself one last look. I could see the reflection of unhappiness shining back at me. I had hurt her. I had cut the ties she had with me, causing a suffering on both sides.

"Yes, you did," I lied, continuing on. "Stay away from me and there won't be a problem. I was wrong to try to help you through your nightmare. It won't happen again." I made myself sound angry as I scowled at her. If she could tell that I was lying, she wasn't saying anything. Instead, she took a couple more unnerving steps back until she hit the island. I caught the look of shame right as she turned on her heels and headed for her bedroom.

I wanted to feel bad, and I did maybe just a little bit, but I knew better than anyone that if I allowed her in there would be no letting her go. This was a job, a favor to Zerro, a temporary arrangement. Plus I couldn't do this to her or to myself.

I pushed off the granite countertop reaching into my pocket. I needed out and the only way to get out was to take a job. I gritted my teeth. I would have to call Bree and Tegan. I would have to beg for them to come and look out for her while I got my shit together.

You're doing the right thing.

The voice in my head was a whisper, but I knew it was right. Logging into the driving system, I picked a route for an hours' time.

I hesitated with my thumb in the air over my sister's name. It had been weeks since I last spoke to her since I last called her. I was a dick and a super shitty brother. Picking my balls up off the floor, I pushed the button and waited for her to send me to voicemail. I deserved it.

"Holy shit. Has hell actually frozen over?" she said into the phone, answering on the second ring. Clearly, I was wrong when it came to knowing if she was mad or not.

"I know I should be calling you for something else, maybe even to say hi or ask how Gia is doing, but I'm not. I need a favor from you and Tegan." I paused, waiting to see how she would respond to me

"Oh, okay. What's going on?" Concern filled her voice. I tried to tell myself she didn't care, and that it was all a part of my imagination, but I knew that was a lie. No one cared as much as Bree did.

"I'm sure Zerro told you that I'm babysitting. I have Isabella here, and I need some time away if you know what I mean." I paused mid-sentence, wondering how what I had said made me look into my sister's eyes.

"I took a job for the afternoon driving, and I need someone to be here with her. I know you don't owe me anything, but I don't want her here alone. Plus she could use some interaction with other women." Nothing I had said was a lie. All the above was the honest truth.

"Zerro told me all about it. What can we do? Do you want us to have girl time with her?" I could hear Gia giggling in the background. Her laughter always filled me with warmth and made me want things I knew I would never have. I was just a dreamer, incapable of making the things I wanted most in life happen.

"Bring some clothes over. She looks to be your size. You can grab some pizza, maybe a couple of movies and make a day out of it. I don't know. Whatever you girls do in your free time. She needs it. She's been through a lot and living with me is hard enough. Do something to make her feel comfortable here."

Bree laughed softly as if something I had said was funny. "Whatever we girls do in our free time? Are you kidding me? I spend money in my free time."

"Perfect. I will leave some money here. Get her some clothes, some shoes, socks, anything she needs or wants."

"All right. We'll be there in about an hour, maybe two. I have to call Tegan so she can get herself and Taylor ready."

"Okay. That's fine."

"See you soon," she says as she hangs up the phone. Nothing she said sounded as if she was mad or aggravated by the conversation, or the fact that I had failed to talk to her for months. Still, I felt more like a douche for having ignored her phone calls for weeks on end only to then end up calling her for a favor of my own. I was a complete contradiction.

I paced the floor for a short time before heading toward Isabella's room. After all I had just said to her, it didn't make much sense to go and hunt her down... Before I could finish my thought, I was walking down the hall and into her bedroom. When I realized she wasn't in sight, a switch seemed to flick on deep inside of me.

Panic surged through me overriding any and all other emotions. Unsure of where she had gone, I walked throughout the room, glancing over her bed and inside the closet a number of times thinking maybe I had missed her somewhere. Just when I was sure I had lost my ever-loving mind, she crossed the threshold of the bedroom with nothing but a towel on. My lower extremities grew and grew, and fucking grew. My eyes glided over her smooth skin. Anxiety and alarm slipped to the back of my mind as relief and the need to wrap my arms around her consumed me.

My eyes caught the sight of her legs. God, they seemed to go on for miles and miles. Water droplets clung to her skin and I wanted to lick them off. Hell, I wanted to be them. I was envious—so fucking envious. The need to caress her skin with my tongue, to see if she would scream my name as I had imagined she would be almost too much.

"Is everything okay?" she asked, clenching her towel as she tried to hide as much of herself from my eyes as possible. The way she was looking at me only made me think dirtier thoughts. My eyes managed to find hers after what seemed like minutes. How could she still look at me as if she cared about my well-being after all I had done to her? The way I had talked, the harshness in which I spoke, the things that I had said...

She should hate me. Not looking at me as if I had saved the day by speaking to her. I almost forgot what it was I had wanted to say, but then I managed to pull myself together.

"I just wanted to let you know that I'm leaving. My

INVINCIBLE

sister and her friend are going to come over while I'm gone so you can have some girl time." I spat the words at her while running like a bat out of hell from her bedroom. I had insulted her, ogled her, and tormented her all within the last hour.

"Wait..." She said softly, her voice like a wisp of the wind in the leaves. I turned around even though I knew I shouldn't have. My eyes caught her in a terrifying stare. In her eyes, I saw a fragile being, one that was incapable of being broken any more than she already was. The pieces of her heart lay shattered on the floor.

"I'm sorry if I'm inconveniencing you." Her teeth sank into her bottom lip nervously. I wanted her. I wanted her lip in between my teeth. I wanted to bite it, to suck on it. To lick it.

"If I'm making living in your own home harder, I can leave..." At the mere words, I wanted to lash out, my cock coming to attention while anger washed over me. *Leave?* Was she secretly doing drugs that I wasn't aware of? Had I come off as that big of an asshole this entire time?

I picked my next set of words very carefully, not wanting to scare her away but not wanting to coddle her either. "See, that's the thing about you." I stepped into her space. "You're not even aware of the danger that lies ahead of you. I don't want you to leave." My breath fell against her cheek. "What I want is to fuck you. To be a part of you in every way that I can, and I know that's not what you need right now. So pardon me for protecting you." A gasp escaped her plump lips. I felt my hands unclenching, the desire to grip her and pin her against the wall. To take her under with me, to show her the true meaning of my darkness.

Her eyes grew large, and I couldn't even tell what it was that lingered inside them. Fear. Excitement. I didn't even know, and instead of trying to determine it what it was, I took a step back and then another until I was no longer in her vicinity, no longer in the house and no longer within distance of reaching out to her. I couldn't be in the same room or area as she was right now. She made me think things that were irrational and straight up crazy.

When I came home tonight, she would be asleep and my life would be easier for another eight hours. Air filtered into my lungs as I started my Tahoe and headed out of the driveway pulling onto the street. I would wait until Bree and Taylor got here before leaving.

CHAPTER NINE

Isabella

HIS ADMISSION SEEMED to frighten me but only slightly as I had never been with a man before, and while that fear was self-explanatory, I still felt my body heating and a flush growing across my skin.

I opened my mouth to try to respond to what he had said, but not only would the words not come out, but I also saw he had turned around and was heading toward the garage. I couldn't leave things like this between us—but, then again, what would I have said anyway? Each time I tried to say something he would have a more powerful retort. As if he kept it on the tip of his tongue waiting for the perfect moment to let it out.

I understood the lustful expressions he was giving me. The men in the trades had given me the same looks on numerous occasions. Things were different when Jared gazed at me, though. He watched me like a man thirsty for water, not like a piece of property or meat.

He didn't make me feel used or filthy. If anything, I felt wanted and needed, something inside of him calling to that black hole inside of me.

I had never wanted a man, let alone wanted one to touch me, but with Jared, it was different. I felt a spark when he looked at me, my body awakening at just the mere thought of him. Even if he was broody most of the time, there still was something about him, something that lingered under the surface. Maybe it was a longing to be understood, to be accepted as is. In all truths, we both did, and I think it was the force underneath it all. It's where we came together. It was more than being the missing piece to one another's puzzles—it was about connecting.

Clutching the towel to my body, I cleared my mind. Pushing the feelings of coldness and loneliness away. I slipped the towel from my body and dried off before using it to wrap my hair in a twist so it could dry.

Stepping into a pair of sweats and a t-shirt given to me by the FBI caused a desire to form within me. Oh, how I longed for something that was my own. Something that said Isabella and was just mine. Growing up in Russia, and being considered a low-income family, I never had that. My clothes were my mother's hand me downs being passed from generation to generation. Sometimes, if Mother had a few extra coins after taking care of the important things we needed, then she would take me to a thrift store and let me get one or two pieces of clothing. But they were never mine, they were still someone else's and eventually, they would become one of my siblings.

"Isabella…" I heard my name being called and found myself scrambling from the bedroom. I wasn't ready to meet anyone else. Friends weren't a luxury I had in the trades. Getting close to the other girls was a grave mistake. For when the time came for them to be taken away, you were left feeling more alone than you had been before.

"Here." My voice was meek. I looked down at myself, running my palms over the material of my shirt before entering the living room knowing that I wasn't really dressed for company.

"Goodness." A woman with dark hair gasped, her reaction making me even more uneasy.

Standing beside her was a little girl who had wrapped her little arms around the woman's leg as soon as they stopped. She smiled up at me with excitement in her eyes, and I couldn't help but smile at her. She was so innocent and a part of me longed to be that young and carefree again.

"Tegan, you need to get in here stat," the woman yelled out the front door that had been left wide open. I wondered what was going on when the girl she had referred to as Tegan walked through the door with a baby stuck to her hip and carrying a bunch of bags, with logos I didn't recognize on them, in her free hand. Her hair was bright red like fire and when she smiled, it reached her eyes, telling me that she was sincere, happy.

"Isabella." The dark haired woman finally greeted me. "This is Tegan, my best friend and our two daughters, Gia and Taylor. Oh, I'm Bree, Jared's sister. He sent us over to hang out with you for a little bit while he does some work." Her face was heartfelt, and as she looked at me, I could see she felt empathy for me but not pity. More so as if she was sorry I had been through what I had. I wanted to tell her she had no reason to feel that way but kept my lips sealed,

INVINCIBLE

knowing that maybe she had her own reasons for feeling the way she did.

"It's nice to meet you both," I spoke softly, showing my manners as Bree bent down and whispered something in her daughter's ear. I watched as Gia nodded her head and then sat on the carpet in the center of the living room while Bree handed her a cup. She took small sips as Bree turned around and grabbed the bags out of Tegan's hand. I hadn't asked for anything since I was delivered here, so I stayed rooted in the same spot, hesitant as to what they had brought with them.

"Jared said you needed some clothes and girl stuff, so we brought you different things," Bree stated as she talked with her hands, seeming far too happy to be helping me. Tegan closed the front door and then placed her daughter on the floor next to Bree's daughter. My gaze drifted to the girls and then finally to the bags that were in Bree's hand.

"We got you some clothes, the common stuff like jeans and different style tops. I even snuck a couple of summer dresses and shorts in there for you," she stated as she pulled items out of the bags, placing them on the couch before me. They were an array of vibrant colors, all the material appearing to be soft. Tears were forming behind my eyes as I stared at them in awe. They looked so beautiful that I wondered if I was even good enough to wear them.

"Oh, and I got you some decent sandals plus some socks and undies." Bree smiled at me as she continued on with her sentence. I returned the smile knowing I should be more than grateful for what they had done. It was apparent she hadn't just done it for Jared but because she wanted to.

"Thank you." I choked out the words, emotions overwhelming me. They had no idea what they had done for me.

"No, no. Thank you," Bree said softly, and I almost didn't catch it. I didn't know what she was thanking me for, but whatever it was must have been important to her.

"We also brought chocolate… because it's every girl's best friend. And we got you female stuff for when that time comes, so you don't have to ask Jared to get those personal things." Tegan reached forward, slowly grabbing my hand as she placed a bar wrapped in gold colored wrapping in my palm. *Chocolate.* I had heard the word many times, but only ever tasted the stuff once or twice when I was younger.

"Let's not forget the wine. We know you haven't had the best time since being found, and we figured we could give you a couple of things that always make us feel better," Tegan confessed causing a small giggle to leave my throat. The way these two cared for others was amazing. They didn't even know me, had never even met me before this moment yet they were standing here showing me compassion. It was no wonder why Jared had asked them to come and care for me while he was gone.

"Thank you so much for bringing me this stuff. I'm not used to having others to talk to, so please excuse my quietness. I'm truly thankful for you both."

They both turned to one another, giving each other a look, and then back to me, bright smiles marring their faces.

"Truthfully, it's an honor," Bree said sincerely, crossing the room as she wrapped me in a warm embrace. I stood there very still for a moment and then lifted my own arms, unsure if I should hug her back or not. She pulled away before I could make the decision and guilt hit me. I should've hugged her back.

"If you need anything, let me know..." she whispered, and then walked away leaving me with my own swarming thoughts. I watched them both as they made themselves at home. I didn't know what to do, so I thanked them both again and took the bags they had brought me back to my bedroom. Once there, curiosity got the best of me, and I decided to take a peek inside one of the bags that Bree hadn't opened in front of all of us. Pulling the bag open, I caught sight of a pair of red lace undies. My heartbeat spiked, and my mind went into overdrive trying to figure out why she would've gotten these.

With nimble fingers, I plucked them from the bag. I stared at them for a moment before running my fingers over the intricate pattern of lace. I had never felt something so soft or seen something so intimately made. I drew a lazy circle across the pattern again, my mind beginning to wonder... What would Jared think of these?

Stop, I told myself right away, not allowing the thought to process any further. Placing the undies back in the bag, I took a couple deep breaths and then decided it was best to head back into the living room.

Once there I noticed the girls were now sitting on a blanket with toys surrounding them as they laughed and giggled with each other while Bree and Tegan had the bottle of wine open and two glasses had been filled with a gold bubbly liquid. I had never had wine before, and a part of me was nervous to indulge, even experience the effects that alcohol would have on me. I wanted to feel free, but how could I be when I knew there were others out there just like I had once been? I knew I had to learn to live with what happened, and if I stayed as I was, I would always be half the person I wanted to be. I didn't want that, but I also couldn't just wash the guilt away as if it wasn't there.

"Cheers." Bree grinned, handing me a wine glass before reaching into her purse for a bottle of water. I looked at her, wondering why she wasn't drinking with us. She must have caught the question written on my face because she answered without me even asking.

"I'm pregnant… again, so no wine for me," she stated with a smile on her face as Tegan and I toasted our glasses against her bottle of water.

"Congratulations," I responded, Bree's thank you for coming shortly after. I watched them each take a sip of their drinks as I sat there, hesitating to do the same.

"It's okay to be happy, Izzy. You don't mind if I call you Izzy, do you?" Tegan questioned. I stared at her shaking my head no. She was beautiful in every way possible. A sprinkle of freckles marked her cheeks, her lips a ruby red matching her hair.

"Don't feel ashamed to be living. I know what you went through is something none of us would ever be able to imagine, but we all have had our experiences, each one just slightly different from the next. You, me, even Bree, so know that we are here for you and there is life after everything you went through."

Tegan's words soothed me in ways she would never truly understand. I didn't know their stories or how they came to be who they were, but the more I sat here and listened to them talk to one another, the more I wanted to.

"Zerro, I mean, Agent King, the one who rescued you is my husband. That is our daughter, Gia." She pointed to the dark beauty on the floor, and I smiled at the fact that I had assumed right. "That is Taylor, Tegan's daughter. Teg here is married to Devon, someone my family will always be indebted to, as well. He's also my husband's partner and friend." As Bree said her name, Taylor turned around staring at me. Her eyes were a bright blue, so blue I wondered how they could even be real. She had short red hair while Gia had dark brown eyes and curly locks that covered her head.

"Your daughters are beautiful," I mustered up the courage to say. Looking at them, I couldn't help but feel pangs of guilt. Those other women they were daughters, cousins, maybe even mothers. Their lives had been ripped from them just as mine had been and here I was sitting on a couch enjoying the simple joys of life.

"I know that look. Don't let the guilt take you under, or you'll never be able to break free of the pain that you've endured," Bree whispered into my ear, her hand touching my own. Her touch was meant to calm me, to remind me I was here and no longer there—with them.

"I'm okay…" I lied unsure of how to explain the guilt I was feeling. There was no real way to explain it, no words that could bring the image to life, at least not in a way that they would understand. Even though I was free, I knew someone else would take my place. Someone else would become a captive with no choice of who they gave their bodies to.

"You don't have to lie. Believe me, I know what not being okay looks like. I know what it feels like to hurt." Bree's voice was sincere as I forced a weak smile.

"We all have our secrets. Some so dark we're afraid that others would look at us differently if they saw them. Never be afraid to admit that." Bree's words cradled me, almost as if she had the power to take the pain away. It was as if she understood the demons that plagued my soul.

Lost in the words Bree had spoken, I hadn't realized Tegan had come and gone until she came from outside with more bags. She handed them to me, and I took them, whispering another thanks as I sat my glass down on the table and got up, walking to my room slowly.

Placing the bags on the bed, I took a seat next to them. I needed a second to catch my thoughts, to place everything back where it belonged.

I wanted to go back out to the living room and socialize, become friends and make memories I had never had before. I wanted to know these two women's stories, and for the first time, I wanted to share mine. I wanted to confide in someone without worrying if I would ever get the chance to do so again. Plus, staying in my room contemplating life wouldn't be fair to them, especially after the way they had treated me.

Standing up, I walked back out of my room toward the living room. Tegan and Bree were talking softly as I made my way down the hall. I could hear Jared's name being spoken, and it forced me to stop right outside the entryway, listening intently.

"He's never called me. I mean he has, but it's been months, Teg. *Months*. I really feel like Isabella might be the one thing he needs to set him free of whatever it is that's holding him back. I don't know why. Call me crazy if you want, but I feel it in my heart." There was sadness in Bree's voice that caused my own heart to ache. She cared for her brother—that much was true.

There was a small pause, Gia and Taylor's sounds

filling the silence before Tegan responded. "Hey, I don't think you're crazy but listen to me. He has his own reasons for hurting. Just like you did, Zerro did, Devon and even I did. We all deal with things differently. Izzy, she's something special for sure. Neither one of them may see it, but she is already changing him. The Jared we have seen these last three years would have never invited us over. He would have left her here and not cared. He cares for her even if he doesn't want to acknowledge it. They are two broken people, just like all of us were." Tegan paused briefly before carrying on. "Just remember, two broken people have the power to bring one another together, or they have enough power to take everyone and everything out. Destruction. Mayhem. Even love rests in their hands." Tegan spoke far wiser than her age as if she understood what true brokenness really was.

I turned my back against the wall, my hands clutching my chest. The way they spoke told me they had pasts, they had walked somewhere in the darkness all on their own. I didn't know how they came to be or where they were from. They could've had the same upbringing as I had or worse. Just because they hid their pain better than me didn't mean they weren't hurting.

"You're right. I just hope the light I see inside of Isabella can pull Jared from the darkness that has surrounded him. If she can't, then I don't think there is any saving him." Bree sounded so defeated that I could feel the sadness as it seeped into the room. It was then I wondered what had caused Jared so much pain.

What caused him to push everyone he loved away?

CHAPTER TEN

Jared

MUSIC BLARED FROM somewhere inside the house, the beat causing the front door to vibrate as my mind wondered what exactly Bree and Tegan had done to Isabella. Had they transformed her? Had they caused her to lose touch with the reality of her dreams that plagued her?

Without another thought, I unlocked the front door and pushed through it. Rihanna's S&M instantly rattling my eardrums. Isabella was nowhere in sight, so I closed the door quietly behind me and headed further into the house. The music grew louder as I got closer to the hallway. I was just about to head toward my bedroom when a blur formed before me as her body slid right past me. My eyes were still directed to the floor, to the pair of sock covered feet before me. Then they were gliding up her body, taking in the fact that her legs were bare.

Completely fucking bare.

INVINCIBLE

Holy. Fucking. Shit.

They were tan and smooth—and long, and… *Fuck!* Was I drooling? I wanted to grab one and wrap it around my waist as I caressed the silkiness of her skin.

A squeak filled the air as she noticed me, yet my attention was still on her legs. By the time I made it up to the hem of the shirt she was wearing, which happened to be mine, I was panting. Ready to fucking devour her in every way imaginable. She looked up at me innocently, her cheeks growing a shade darker than usual.

"I didn't…" She stumbled over her words, which just caused my dick to grow painfully harder. "I mean, I did know what I was doing, but I didn't…" She attempted to talk again only to mumble the last bit of her sentence. She looked timid, maybe even a little afraid, but still there was a look of lust in her eyes that had me wondering if she was as innocent as she played herself out to be.

I cleared my throat before talking, knowing she would be able to tell from my voice that I had a desire to taste her, to touch her, to bring every single dream I had ever had about her to life.

"Why are you wearing my shirt, and why the fuck were you in my bedroom?" I covered the need with anger because there was no way I could allow her to burrow herself any deeper into my life, my feelings or my fucking head.

"I just wanted…" She looked lost for words, and suddenly, I started to feel like an even bigger dickhead. I had treated her like shit since she arrived, and though it was for her own good, I needed to cut the shit. I needed to be protecting her and making her feel safe. With all she had been through, she deserved a sliver of happiness in her dark life.

"I'm... I'm fucking sorry. Okay?" I ran my fingers through my hair, sighing. I wasn't sure what the hell I was supposed to say to her to make her feel better. Apologizing wasn't really my thing. I knew this was wrong—I knew that Zerro picked the wrong person when it came to her. She needed more than I could ever give her.

"Okay. I just saw a girl in one of the shows on TV that I was watching with Bree and Tegan earlier. She wore her boyfriend's dress shirt—not saying you are my boyfriend but anyway, she danced around the house. I just didn't know you were coming home so early. I'm really sorry." Her words were so sincere, I could almost feel myself cracking. I wanted to cradle her, to protect her in ways I shouldn't.

"No. No, it's all right. I just..." Just what? What was I going to come up with? Another excuse for why I was being a dick? I mean, I couldn't just come out and say 'I want to stick my cock deep in your pussy.' *God no.* That would be just crude. "I just wasn't expecting it is all. It took me by surprise. I haven't ever had a woman wear my clothing before." My body was acting of its own accord as I took a step forward, coming into her space. I drank in her scent and the way her body reacted to my own as my fingers reached out to push a lock of her dark hair out of her face.

God, I wanted her. I had never wanted a woman so badly. She looked up at me, her eyes growing wide with lust and a desire unfamiliar to even her. In an instant, I had her in my arms. I was holding her to my body, her curves molding to my hardness in the most perfect of ways.

"I really am sorry. I didn't mean to make you

angry." She tried to get the words out, but they were muffled against my shirt as I gripped her tighter. My eyes drifted closed as I thought over my next words. Was there an excuse for me touching her?

"Never be sorry. God, don't be fucking sorry. It's I who should be sorry." I cursed myself for allowing the admission to fall from my lips.

She pulled away from me, confusion marring her face. "I don't understand what you mean? You're mad, right? I mean, I didn't mean to cause you to be mad, but I just wanted to try this once, and I never expected you to come home..." Her voice fell from my mind. All I could see were her lips moving and then I was descending upon her. My hands cupped the sides of her cheeks as my lips sought hers.

The moment they touched one another's was when silence consumed her. I could tell the second she understood what was taking place. I could feel her walls falling and her mind opening up to me. Her hands clung to me as I softly nibbled on her bottom lip. That full bottom lip had been the death of me over the past few days.

A soft purr left her throat and I smiled like a sick son of a bitch as my lips moved against hers in the softest, slowest strokes I had ever made. She gathered her own rhythm and pressed herself firmly against me, her grip growing tighter as the seconds flew by. I envisioned placing her on my bed and ripping my shirt away, possessing her body in every way that I possibly could.

Still I forced myself to release her, knowing that if I kept touching her or allowing her to touch me—hell, if I had to continue to stare at her in this way, we wouldn't be leaving this spot without something happening.

With more restraint than I knew I ever had, I released her, stepping back until I was out of touching distance. She looked at me with a pout on her face, her bottom lip out a bit more than her top lip. My cock grew harder with every passing second.

"I'm not the good guy in all of this, but even I know when enough is enough." I paused, taking a deep breath before I allowed my next sentence to come out. "I just couldn't go another day without at least knowing what you tasted like. I needed to know what you felt like under my hands, what your skin felt like against mine." The words were nothing that I had ever felt or said aloud to another person before. Her expression turned to shock right away and then a soft smile formed on her face.

"Does this mean we can be friends?" Her question was so naïve. What about, I want to fuck you until you can't walk straight said I want to be friends? Yeah, maybe with your pussy.

I shook my head. "I thought we already were friends?" I raised an eyebrow up at her. I couldn't blame her if she said we weren't. I had been the biggest jackass on the face of the planet. The truth was while I was away at work, I couldn't stop thinking about her. Even though I left the house to get away, I longed to be here. Hell, I hardly knew her so I could chalk it up to being alone for so long. But the reality was I craved someone who understood what it was like to be alone.

"We were, I mean, we are." She corrected herself, standing taller. The way she talked and acted and simply based on her past experiences I knew I needed to find a way to protect her when I wasn't around. She might not be here forever, but when she left, I wanted to make sure she took something good away from this entire experience.

"Isabella." Her name rolled off my tongue so smoothly it was almost impossible to tell it was once foreign to me. A small voice in the back of my mind said, it's because it's not foreign.

"Jared..." My mother's singsong voice entered my ears.

The memory was jarring causing me to take another step back. Maybe my anger toward Isabella had nothing to do with her but everything to do with what she reminded me of.

"Jared," Isabella called my name and my eyes lifted to meet hers. Alarms were going off in my head telling me I needed to push her away, to make her believe my desire for her had everything to do with finding comfort in someone's flesh. Yet, as I formed the sentences in my mind, I couldn't force myself to say them.

"Are you okay?" Again, her voice soothed the chaos brewing within me. She took a step toward me, and I could feel my hard exterior cracking.

No. Never again.

The words hung in the air. *I couldn't. We couldn't. It was too good to be true.*

"I'm fine. I just wanted to let you know I'm going to take you out to the gun range so I can teach you how to shoot." I kept my voice neutral as I felt myself drawing back into my shell.

The expression that formed on her face told me she wasn't expecting that. My nonchalant attitude had hurt her. Dolefulness filled her features and in an instant disappeared.

"Oh, okay. That sounds great," she said it sounded great, yet her voice made it sound like I had just cut her deep and then spit on her. I backed up, not sure where to go from here. I had made out with her, felt her up, and now I was giving her the cold shoulder again.

She had no idea what kind of fucked up I was. She had no idea that it wasn't she who was the problem, but me.

All me. Always fucking me.

I couldn't drag her through the dirt and mud, tainting her with the mess I had made out of my own life. With one last glance over my shoulder, I walked away, my footsteps deafening against the ground as if there was a hidden meaning behind them. It was as if every step I took away from her was causing a rift to grow between us.

How was it one girl could cause everything to crumble that I had spent years building?

She didn't know her worth. She didn't know the power she had over me, and I hoped she never would, because the second she did was the second there would be no saving either of us from the destruction I would cause.

CHAPTER ELEVEN

Isabella

"I WISH BOSS would let us fuck 'em." The man's words rung in my ear. I could still feel his breath hot against my skin as his hand explored my body in ways that I never even had.

"You're a monster," I whispered. I could hear his muffled laughter against my cheek. He lifted his face to stare down at me, preparing to beat me or punish me. I didn't know.

"You're just as disgusting as she was." The meaning behind his words was hidden, but the complete disgust in his voice told me whoever 'she' was, wasn't someone he liked.

"Isabella." My name was being called. The voice was thick and smooth, a voice I would love to get wrapped up in breaking through my past.

"You're having another nightmare. Wake up." *Jared?* The recognition took root, and immediately, I sat up on the bed, cradling my blanket to my body. I blinked my eyes open only to discover Jared was in fact standing at the foot of my bed. His chest was bare, and he looked less than pleased that I had woken him up from his slumber.

"Goodness, I'm so sorry," I said nervously. Jared had that effect on me. It didn't matter what time of the day it was, or what I was doing. He caused a nervous tick to form in my body, one that only came on when he was near.

He scrubbed a hand down his face and over the light stubble that marred it. His hair was a mess, giving way to just how asleep he was.

"You know if you wanted a cuddle buddy that bad, all you had to do was say something." He sighed, dropping down to the right side of the bed. I was still recovering from being awakened. I didn't realize what he had said or what it was he was doing.

"What are you talking about?" I almost yawned but stopped myself. It was when I felt his warmth against me underneath the blankets that I realized what he was getting at. Turning, I looked at him with a shocked expression written on my face.

"What are you doing?" I questioned. This wasn't supposed to happen again. No, there was no way it was supposed to happen again, it couldn't.

"Making sure you don't have any more nightmares." He stated nonchalantly as he pulled me down into his chest. Was I so weak that I wouldn't even protest against it?

"You know you could just buy me some lights to hang in here. It would be less…" I paused looking for the exact word to use, but my mind drifted just as Jared's hand did. *My hip. His hand.* I almost couldn't form a thought.

"Less what?" He whispered into my ear, causing goose bumps to erupt all over my skin. I could no longer remember what it was that I was going to say.

"Less…" I stuttered. "Damaging. Exhausting. Embarrassing." The words left me without mere thought. I could feel his body tensing. Was he upset with me?

"I'll get some lights, but for now, you're stuck with me." He sounded so sure of himself and I almost budged.

"I'll be okay," I whispered on the borderline of giving in. Was I so lonely I would allow him to lay with me, even if it was to calm me after a nightmare?

"You're right. You will be… now that I'm here." He situated me against him, my hips lining up with his groin perfectly. One arm wrapped around me while the other cradled my head. Moments of silence passed between us, the only thing that could be heard were our breaths filling the air. My eyes drifted closed as I allowed the peace of what was taking place to sink into my skin. I wanted to soak up every ounce of joy.

Jared's heartbeat was loud, pounding against my skin. My mind drifted to the kiss we shared in the hall earlier and to the things he said to me. It was as if he wanted two very different things from all of this.

"What causes your nightmares?" His voice was like velvet against my skin. I stayed silent for a moment trying to determine if I should share that with him. It was intimate to me. A secret really, and if others found out they could use it against me.

"The darkness," I finally answered. Silence formed between us again, and I wondered if he had fallen asleep, and then he answered me.

"There's a dark side to everything in life." His

words told me he understood the real meaning of darkness.

"Even you?" I questioned, unsure where the question even came from.

"Yes, even me. Even the brightest of people have a small part of them they keep hidden away from everyone, a dark hole that eats away at them piece by piece." It was in what he said that I understood what tormented him. He was confessing his pain, his griefs without even admitting them to me.

"Your secret is safe with me," I muttered, allowing my eyes to drift closed. I could feel his breath on my neck and it caused me to fall deeper and deeper into a comatose state. Right before I fell off the cliff of darkness, I swear I heard him say 'thank you.'

* * * * *

The next morning played out very similar to the first. It was awkward and even though he was a bit eager to get away from me, he hadn't run from me this time—that alone caused my heartbeat to skyrocket.

He wanted to touch me in ways a man had never been allowed to, and I wanted to let him, solely because I felt safe with him. I felt desired, and though he showed it strangely, I felt cared for.

For someone to have that kind of hold over someone else's emotions showed how much power they had over you. It was clear as day he had that type of power over me. I showered and dressed while he made breakfast, and as I braided my hair, my nose caught a whiff of coffee in the air. *And was that bacon?*

Once I was finished with my hair, I allowed the smell to guide me into the kitchen. As I closed in on

Jared, I couldn't remove my eyes from his body. His dark hair was a mess all over his head and his attention was focused on cooking breakfast.

His black shirt clung to his body, and for the first time in my life, I was jealous of another person's shirt. *Especially his.* It got to rub against him, cling to his muscles, his abs, and his skin.

"Morning," he said gruffly, pulling me from my ogling stare.

"Morning," I replied, feeling as if I had been caught doing something wrong as I took a seat at the table. Not that staring was wrong—one couldn't help it when someone that good looking was right in front of you. More so the thoughts that were swirling around inside of my head when I was staring at him.

He shot me a smile, relating my thoughts to his as he placed a plate of food in front of me. I smiled back at him, digging into my food right away. Anything to keep my mouth from running.

"Were going to the gun range today. I found some old lights down in the basement, so when we get home, I'll set them up for you." Food caught in my throat and I almost gasped for air. *Did he just say gun range?*

"Gun range?" I asked in confusion. He shot me an evil smile, one that should've scared me. Instead, it caused my blood to sing loudly and my heartbeat to pound in my ears.

"Don't you remember what I told you last night? I want to teach you how to shoot a gun. Not only is it important for a woman to know how to do so, but it's important to be able to protect yourself in general. Especially in a case where your attacker may be able to out power you. Having and knowing how to use a gun correctly could ultimately save your life."

INVINCIBLE

He wanted to put the power back in my hands. I told myself day in and day out that I wasn't a victim, but a survivor. Since being rescued, it was all I had been doing. *Surviving*. I wasn't really living because I was afraid of what was lurking on the other side of the door. I needed to move forward. But how could someone move forward in their life when they were afraid of change, of people or simply the dark?

"I...." I wasn't sure what I had wanted to say. I couldn't tell him no because, even if guns scared me, they had protected me back when those FBI agents swooped in and saved us. For every good thing, there was an evil one to everything in my life.

He eyed me hesitantly before sliding off his chair and coming to stand next to me. "I know it's scary, and that everything in your life is scary right now, but I can't allow you to stay here and not know how to protect yourself. If you don't do it for yourself, then at least do it for me... Because if something ever happened to you, and I knew there was something that I could've done, I would never forgive myself." As my eyes met his, I felt the sentiment in his words and knew they were true.

I would be the reason for his downfall, and instead of bringing him back from the darkness, I would be sending him deeper into it. I needed to give him this peace of mind. I nodded my head, signaling I would go, even if it were just for him.

Silence consumed both of us as we cleaned the dishes from breakfast. Once done, I went back into my room and slipped my boots on as Jared grabbed the keys.

I followed him out into the garage, all the while watching him pull his leather jacket on. This was the one place in the house I had never been before, I thought as I took in the two cars parked side by side. I panicked as he headed for the bike that was off to the left. I would never in a million years get on that thing.

"We aren't taking that, are we?" I asked, looking at him as if he had grown two heads.

"Oh, yes, we are, Isabella," he said grinning as if he fed off my terror. I stopped dead in my tracks just short of the bike. It was black and sleek, and I wondered if it sparkled in the sunlight.

"Are you scared?" I could feel his breath on my neck as he reached around me to start it. My body reacted to his voice and the sound of the motor roaring to life. Terror consumed me, but underneath it was curiosity. A need to know if it would vibrate under my thighs and how my body would feel wrapped around his as the wind blew through my hair and against my skin. Would it be like flying?

He placed his hands on my hips, skimming his fingers over my skin causing me to bite my lip in reaction. God, I had never wanted to moan out in pleasure so much in my life.

"I promise I'll go nice and slow...." His voice was sex on a stick as he lightly lifted me from my feet, placing me on the back of his bike.

Pulling my hair back, I allowed him to place a helmet on my head and then he was sliding in front of me causing our bodies to glide against one another's. The friction alone caused a spark, a flame of fire to ignite between the two of us.

"Hold onto me, Izzy baby," he yelled as he revved the engine his voice being drowned out by the noise. Doing as he said I gripped onto him, my hands sliding underneath his jacket and onto his stomach. The second

INVINCIBLE

my fingers made contact with his chiseled abs was the second I felt like I would die a happy woman. *Lord, please help me.*

My chest collided with his back as he pulled out of the garage. As soon as the garage door came down, he pulled away from the house like a bullet flying out of the barrel of a gun. The air whipped across my exposed skin in a rush. I had never felt so much freedom in my entire life. Our bodies clashed with the momentum of the bike.

I could feel my body being lifted as the power from the engine pushed us forward. I gripped onto Jared like a lifeline, afraid if I didn't, the wind would carry me away. My chest filled with air as we took a sharp turn out onto the highway. My nails dug into his skin at the unexpected movement, and I swear I could hear him groan.

My thighs clung to his in a manner that was doing crazy things to my head. Every time we sped up, those crazy thoughts just grew wilder.

By the time we made it to the gun range, my whole body was warm all over. The second he parked, I unglued myself from him and got off the bike, not knowing if I would attack him right here, right now. *Get a grip, Isabella.*

I pulled the helmet off my head and handed it to him, expecting him to take it. What I didn't expect was for him to reach out and brush back the loose strands of hair that had escaped from behind my ear. He had a way with his touch—each caress of his fingers against my skin or hair made me feel that much more engulfed in him.

"You're beautiful." The words slipped from his mouth with ease as if he had thought it over a thousand times. From the look on his face, it was apparent that even he wasn't aware he was saying such things until they were already out. His admission was truthful and full of emotions I had never seen before.

"Thank you," I offered, unsure what else I should say to him. I couldn't just say you're beautiful, too. Or could I?

Securing my hand in his, he pulled me toward the door of the building. It looked like an abandoned warehouse. The sidings were brown, and there was a giant glass door mirroring my reflection in front of us with a tiny overhead hanger to shield those entering in from the rain.

I watched as Jared pulled out a key card, slipping it into the door to gain entry. For a brief moment, I wondered why he had such a card and then I took in my surroundings. I wanted to panic, to explode. I couldn't do this. I was trapped inside with no way out. Jared must've felt a change in my demeanor because he turned around, cupping my cheek in one of his hands.

"Don't think. Don't allow your fears to rule you." His voice calmed me, putting me into what felt like a trance as I allowed him to guide me through a pair of doors and into an open room that looked like a waiting room with tables and chairs placed everywhere.

With little effort, he pulled me across the room, sliding his card once again to gain access to the next set of doors. Once inside, we entered a large room that was far bigger than the other one we had been in only moments ago. I took in the entire room within a couple of seconds, my eyes zeroing in on the far wall that was lined with guns of all types and sizes.

Anxiety formed in me and I felt myself backing up toward the door. Jared saw the worry within me and in

INVINCIBLE

an instant took a step toward me.

"Guns are used to protect you. Yes, they have the potential to hurt you but so does anything in life." Everything he said held truth, but the panic inside of me was constantly rising. I had heard gunshots in the trades. I had heard screams and pleas for mercy. When I thought of guns, I thought of what they could bring. *Death.*

"I don't want to do this, Jared. It reminds me too much of them..." Dread filled my voice as I took another step back. Jared's arms wrapped around me in an instant, his fingers splaying across my back causing an eruption of emotions to form within me.

"You're bigger than your biggest fears." He soothed. I placed my head against his chest, focusing on the beat of his heart. Was he right? Could I get over my own fears? Before I could answer my own question, Jared's voice pulled me back to the here and now.

"Your fears are as big as you allow them to be. If you make them the size of a house, then they will be huge forever, and you'll always have one hell of a time getting over them. But if you make them the size of a small stone, then you can easily overcome them."

He gripped my chin forcing me to look up into his eyes and nowhere else. It was in those eyes that I saw someone who had greater fears than I ever did. Someone who was on a path of destruction. In the depths of those beautiful brown eyes, I saw a person more lost than I ever was, and I wanted to reach right inside of him, pull him out, and offer him everything he needed even if it left me without anything.

"Ready?" he asked pulling me from my thoughts. Instead of doing that, I nodded my head yes, allowing him to bring me over to the table covered with guns.

"What is this place?" I questioned curiously, eyeing one of the guns.

"It's a shooting range, one that Agent King had made for him and his team. They come here and train, shooting practice basically, every once in a while. I have free range to use it whenever, so here we are." His voice was placid as he picked up a gun, one that had caught my eye. It was small, sleek, and black, and I wondered how such a small weapon could take someone's life.

"Really? That's pretty cool. I didn't know that agents could build their own shooting ranges. I mean, it's not like I know a lot of things, but..." God, I sounded so fucking stupid. Jared said nothing, his eyes still glued on the gun he had plucked off the table as I trailed off.

"Let's try this one out. It's small, lightweight, and its accuracy is right on when it comes to hitting its target." With the gun still in his hand, he guided me over to something that looked like a booth. Setting the gun down, he grabbed a pair of earmuffs and what looked like goggles for your eyes, placing them down in front of us.

"Is this going to be hard to shoot?" I asked as my face scrunched up in confusion. I hadn't a clue what I was doing and I hated it. I hated the unknown because it reminded me of the past, of the fact that at one point in time, I didn't know where I would end up.

"No, it's pretty easy. The black part right here..." He pointed toward the part of the gun that he held against his palm, "holds your ammunition. It's called a magazine." With the flick of his finger, he discharged what he called the magazine, causing some of the ammunition to release from the bottom.

Then as fast as he had discharged it, he slipped it

back in, a loud click filling the room. From there, he showed me the components of the gun, how to check if it's loaded, and how to turn the safety on and off. I could feel the sweat on my palms as he placed the goggles on my head and the earmuffs onto my ears, leaving one ear slightly uncovered. My stomach filled with butterflies instantly as he placed me in front of him.

Taking my hand, he placed it against the gun forcing me to grip it, his hand covering my own. I could feel my heartbeat pulsing as his body became flush with mine.

"Safety off." Jared's voice came out calm yet strong and with the flick of my finger, the safety came off. My arms wobbled nervously as I stared at the target against the wall. Would I even hit it? Was there really a reason to learn how to shoot a gun? When would I ever shoot someone? Questions filled my head, spiking my nervousness.

I can't do this I told myself, my palms still sweating profusely almost causing me to lose my grip.

"Aim," he whispered in my ear. We were so close it was as if we were no longer two bodies but one as I could feel his pulse through his shirt.

"Breathe." I could feel my vision blurring, my breaths coming in as heavy pants. "Breathe slowly and shoot," I could hear him say to me, and when my breaths finally evened out, his finger pressed against my own gently on the trigger.

"Fire steady." With stealth and precision, he forced my finger against the trigger. A loud muffled bang echoed around me vibrating through my body and filling the room. My breathing was harsh as the bullet left the barrel, flying toward the target on the other side of the room. My arms were shaking like a leaf in the wind as I watched the bullet penetrate the paper.

We continued to stay standing as we were, and for what reasons, I didn't understand. All I knew was when the bullet came out of the barrel I had felt something take over. I felt like the control was in my hands, as if I controlled my life.

"Thank you," I whispered unto him and it was true, I was more than thankful.

For the first time in my life, I was grateful for a gun, for protection, but most of all, for Jared.

CHAPTER TWELVE

"SIR," ANTONIO'S ANNOYING voice sounded in my ears. I lifted my eyes to his face. I clenched my fists together telling myself it would do me no good to beat his head against the side of the car. Antonio was my nephew. I took him in as a child, teaching him everything he needed to know about the family business.

"What?" I simply stated my tone snide. It had been days since we had any contact with the sellers. I was furious they hadn't fought harder against the FBI. Instead, they allowed her to get away, knowing I had paid a quarter of a million to get her. Not knowing where she was at was driving me insane. She could be anywhere, with anyone. She didn't belong to them. She belonged to me.

"Adam thinks he may have confirmation of a location." I wanted to growl, punch something, even spill blood if need be. He thinks? He better hope it's not just an assumption. Adam was my undercover spy, the man who could slip under the radar without being noticed by anyone.

"Does he now? Tell him to call me. I need to talk to

him about said confirmation and be sure to warn him for me. If he is wrong, I will be forced to remove another finger from his hand." I kept my voice cool. I refused to let the men that worked for me know the waiting game was getting the best of me.

But she is yours.

Those words ran through my mind daily, over and over again reminding me once again something promised to me had slipped right through my fingers.

"Will do, sir," was Antonio's response.

I shifted my attention to the men around me. They were getting ready to go out and do another manhunt for the girl. They all knew better than to question me about anything, let alone what the girl's worth was to me. I had all my best men on this, looking for what was mine, and they wouldn't sleep until I knew where she laid her head at night.

"It's been weeks since I had a taste of good pussy. Monroe County ain't got shit for women." Oliver spoke to Stephen as if he were annoyed that he had to be here as if it was my fault he hadn't found any prime pussy. I should've known when I took these two men on they would be nothing but trouble. Back home in Russia they were notorious bad boys.

"Excuse me..." My voice caused all conversations to heed as I turned and made my way over to Oliver. I could feel him quivering beneath me, and I hadn't even spoken his name. As he should be quivering because I was more than his boss. I was his reason for breathing, his reason for living. Without me, he would be nothing. He owed me for everything he had, and he would worship the fucking ground I walked on until he died.

"Sir, I didn't mean it in a disrespectful way..." I cut him off with a slap to the face. My eyes drifted over the red mark on his face. I loved Oliver like one would love their own child, but I refused to allow him to speak in such a manner in front of me.

"Remember why you're here, son. What it is that you're doing for me. That's what's important, yeah? Not a good taste of pussy. Remember without a reason, without a placement you're good as dead. Do you understand me?" I commanded him to answer me, my voice stern.

He murmured a yes into the air as I turned to face the rest of my men. "All of you remember that unless you dare go up against me." I was losing my cool, all over this girl that I would make a woman. *My woman.*

Thoughts of her continued to drift through my mind, forcing the moment she had been promised to me to come forth as bright as the day before me.

"The deal has been settled. Upon her twenty-first birthday, she will be presented to you as a gift, her virginity intact," Sal announced with a slap on my back. I had never understood why Sal was involved in this business. He had a lovely bride and one-year-old daughter. He was a good-looking man, who worked out and ate healthily. He was exactly the opposite of what you would expect from someone in this business.

"You promise she is to be mine? That she is indeed pure and true?" I questioned further, not fully believing him. Sal had a less than stellar track record. Men had purchased from him before only to find out later on that their merchandise was not up to par.

He smiled. "Would I sell you anything less than perfection?"

My eyes narrowed on him. I had been fooled once by a man that sold me a bride. She was beautiful, elegant, and everything I had ever wanted in a woman,

INVINCIBLE

but she was broken, fractured straight down the middle, and she was far from untouched. I wouldn't go down this road again and try to make something out of nothing. My new bride—she would be everything I was promised or I would take her life.

"She will be presented to you in excellent condition. No wrong doings will be done to her. However..." He paused for a moment as if he were re-evaluating his comment.

"It will cost you extra as I know the men will be in desperate need to unleash a little tension..." I could feel my blood boiling, the desire to end this fucker's life. I had already paid more than half of what was expected of a normal buyer for my down payment and the first transport, and now he wanted more?

"Extra?" I cracked my knuckles watching his eyes grow large. Hadn't he realized all that I was capable of doing?

A nervous laugh left his lips. "Well, you know how they can sometimes be. The extra money would be used for—" I cut him off.

"I don't care what the extra money would be used for. That isn't my concern. Your men and the fact they can't keep their cocks out of the merchandise aren't my problem. Now you, you're—" My temper was on the verge of snapping.

"I meant no harm, truthfully." He stuttered over his words as if he finally understood what I had to say.

"You didn't... But I do," I said sinisterly as I reached into the back of my pants, removing my gun. I lifted the barrel to his head and cocked it as my finger began to squeeze the trigger. There was no room for failure in this life. No room for telling someone what to do and allowing them to get away with not listening.

Sometimes you had to take someone else's life into your own hands.

"Boss?" Antonio called my name as the last images of her I had seen disappeared from my mind.

"What?" I responded in aggravation, coming back to the present with a vengeance. The memory had only made me that much more eager to get my hands on her, to feel her softness beneath my hands, to break her down and make her my little slave as I built her back up.

"Adam has confirmation that she's near French Island. He says his word is bond." He spoke firmly, his voice less annoying to me now that he had information I could actually use.

A smile formed on my face, this was the best news yet. "Good. For his sake, I hope he is right. Call Wyatt. Let him know I have a location for him to check out. Oh, and that I need his *skills* to assist in finding my merchandise."

CHAPTER THIRTEEN

Jared

HER BODY WAS silhouetted in the moonlight, her hair sprawled out beneath her as she withered beneath me. God, she was beautiful I thought as her mouth parted open and a throaty moan filled the air.

"Jared, it's only ever been you," she whispered against my skin as if she were trying to tell me a secret.

"Give it to me," she begged as I held myself above her. I hadn't even touched her yet and she was on the verge of begging me.

"Are you sure?" I growled, barely able to get the question out. She nodded her head at me with so much desire in her eyes that I felt like we were already connected.

"Make love to me," she purred.

"Jared." Huh?

"Jared. We fell asleep on the couch." Isabella's sleep filled voice met my ears, causing me to sit up startled. After spending the day at the shooting range and having lunch together, we came home to relax and watch some TV. Apparently, it meant taking a nap, too. Even worse than all of this was the things I had been dreaming about.

"Jared," Isabella said my name sternly. "Your phone's ringing." I turned my attention to her catching the look on her face. It all but said, is he right in the head? Hell, I didn't even know if I was all here. Shaking my head as if to get the dream and the effect it had over my body out of my mind, I plucked my phone off the coffee table.

I sighed and watched Isabella disappear to give me privacy. Motherfucking Alzerro King the caller ID read. Rolling my eyes, I hit the green answer key.

"Sometimes I think you just like being a douche bag." Those were the first words out of his mouth. Not a hello, how are you this fine evening—just straight to the point bullshit.

"Did you just call to insult me or what?" I asked annoyed, voice groggy with sleep. Had I known it was anything less than an emergency, I wouldn't have answered. He had a life, a good one at that, he needed to worry less about me and focus more on his family.

"Not really. I actually called you because I have some intel and I needed to let you know. I also just felt like calling you. You know, making up for lost time." I could hear the humor in his voice.

"Cut the bullshit, Alzerro. You know how I get about jokes and shit like that. I don't have the time for this." Of course, I was getting frustrated right off the bat. Between my day dreaming about Isabella and the fact I hadn't fucked anyone in over a week, I was close to losing my shit on whoever might piss me off even the slightest bit.

"They know she's here. I don't know how, and I don't know when they're going to make an attack. Hell, at this moment, I'm not sure if they know your exact location or just the places you frequent but you need to be ready." He went from funny and joking to serious and business-like so fast, I had gotten whiplash from the change in his attitude.

That was the thing about Agent King per se—you never knew if he was going to break your neck or cause you to bust your gut in laughter.

"She's being cared for… and protected in the best way possible. You know I wouldn't let anything happen. " I kept my voice low, not wanting Isabella to overhear me. She was just in the other room after all.

"Good. These men don't mess around Jared. They'll kill you both before they let you leave with her. They're as bad as I was in my prime days." I snorted, covering my laughter.

"Yeah, before you started driving a minivan and toting Gia back and forth to ballerina class?" Radio silence formed on the other side of the line, which just caused another snort of laughter to escape.

"Asshole. That's what you are. You don't want anyone to joke with you, but yet you turn around and do it to someone else. You're lucky."

"Why is that?" I tested him, trying to get a rise out of him.

"Because if you weren't my childhood friend and brother-in-law, I would've already had the barrel of my gun pressed against your skull." Gun. That one word brought me back to the current situation, to the immediate danger that we were in. What he said caused something inside of me to wake up. It caused a reminder to go off inside my head. I was supposed to be

INVINCIBLE

protecting Isabella. They generally knew where she was, and if they knew that much, it wouldn't take long for them to find out who she was with, pinpointing our exact location.

"Thanks for the heads up. I'll keep my eyes wide open. Anything I feel you need to know, I'll call you." I hung up the phone, a sudden anger filling me.

Isabella was fragile, like glass. Her past was about to collide with my present, and I wondered if either of us would be able to walk away from this unscathed.

"Who was that?" she asked coming back into the living room. As she watched me curiously, I wondered if she could see through my ulterior motives. I tried to smile, to act unfazed, but I couldn't. For a brief moment, I thought about lying to her but changed my mind knowing that she had the right to know what was taking place… After all, this was her life.

"Agent King. He wanted to check in on you." Fuck. I was lying. Yet, there was no way for me to go about telling her that her life could be in danger. That today could be the final nail in her coffin.

She smiled softly. "Yeah, he's a nice guy. His wife, your sister, is nice, too, and Gia." Her smile seemed to grow bigger. "She is so adorable. How blessed you are to have such a lovely family."

There it was. The kick to the gut. The one that ruined it all for me and reminded me exactly why I shouldn't have the feelings I was having. She wouldn't understand what I was going through, not even if I told her or tried to explain it.

I allowed the air to grow thick with tension, not saying anything because honestly, what was I to say. Creases formed across her brow as she began to chew on her bottom lip. She was worried, concerned even.

"I didn't mean it in an offensive way…" Her voice trailed off. I was past listening. I had allowed her to get under my skin. I had allowed her touch, smell, and even her taste to invade my mind, taking over the parts of my body that made all the logical choices.

When I was around her, I wasn't myself. Or maybe the problem was I was myself and I just didn't want to face it. The reasoning didn't matter. All that did was making it stop.

"Aren't you going to say something? Anything?" she stuttered, my mind having to catch up with her words as I drifted off into my own thoughts.

"What's there to say?" My words came out stiff and defensive. It wasn't her fault I was this way. I was caught at a crossroads. Either one that would kill me to cross or one that would become my saving grace.

I wanted to blame her, but something held me back and kept me from saying those small little words that would push her away because, in reality, I wanted her as close as I could get her—even if it meant her body under mine and her breaths meeting my own.

"You could tell me that you're okay. That whatever Alzerro called you for wasn't bad. That when you kissed me earlier it actually meant something to you." Her hands were on her hips. Her nose was scrunched up in a way that said she was about to lose her shit on me. A smile pulled at my lips. She looked so adorable when she was angry. Then it hit me. What she had said, the kiss...

"The kiss?" I questioned acting as if I didn't even remember it taking place. Which was the biggest lie on the face of the planet. Out of the two times our lips had met, I remembered both as vividly as if I had just removed my lips from hers. Shake it off. She's getting to

INVINCIBLE

you. The warning was clear, but for some reason, I refused to say something that would break her heart.

"Yeah, the one where your lips met mine. The one where you made me feel this strange feeling in my belly." She looked at me as if she had accidently slipped the last part out without thinking.

Fuck. Feelings were becoming involved. "Isabella…" I paused attempting to go about this as easily as possible.

"Don't you dare say it was nothing to you! I felt it. It felt like for the first time in your life you were alive." She had an eagerness to prove me wrong in her eyes and that just stoked the already burning fire inside of me.

"It was nothing though. At least for me." I stood, getting up from the couch to stand in front of her. I wanted to prove to her that whatever she thought was happening between us wasn't.

"You're a woman, I am a man. Naturally, we're attracted to one another. That's all this is. There are no hidden feelings underneath it all. If you're trying to fix me, or come up with a solution, you should give up now. There is a long line of women who have been trying to do that for months now, some even years." God, I was an asshole.

"You're a liar…" She barely got out. I could see the hurt in her eyes, the hardness growing around her heart. Is that what I looked like when they told me my mother had died? I shook my head pushing the thoughts away.

"No, I'm not. You just don't know the difference between a man who wants to get his dick wet and a man who wants to give you his heart. You're naïve, sweet Isabella, and I was just making your life easier for you."

Tears leaked from the sides of her eyes, penetrating my soul.

"You know what, Jared? You have the potential to love someone far greater than anyone does. It's just that you're so afraid of letting someone in. So afraid of feeling anything different from what you currently feel." Her words were laced with pain as they struck me hard upon the chest.

"You know nothing but heartache, sadness, and pain. But you know what the ugly thing about it all is? You think you deserve it."

I clenched my fists, she had no fucking clue how close to home she was hitting. My chest ached as pain seared through it. Her words were like a fucking belt lashing against my heart. She was so right, and I was so not ready to admit it.

"I deserve whatever shit God decides to give me. You know nothing about me, only the things I have allowed you to see, and even then, you only know and feel what I want you to know or feel. So don't act like you fucking know me, because you don't and you never will," I gritted through my clenched teeth.

"Don't push me away..." She sounded defeated, and I was so angry and hurt that I couldn't even look at her.

"In order to push you away, you would've had to be close to me to begin with. I'm just doing you a favor." The truth was I was pushing her away, doing what I had wanted to all along. But this time, my heart was breaking right along with hers. The hate falling from my lips burned me more than it did her. She was worthy of more, better... She needed someone to care for her and this exchange of words proved just how

INVINCIBLE

wrong I was for being that person to do it.

I could feel her eyes on me for a few more seconds before her footfalls met my ears. She was walking away, leaving. As she should.

She didn't deserve this.

Only I did.

CHAPTER FOURTEEN

Isabella

MY TEETH SANK hard into my bottom lip as I attempted to force the tears away. These feelings swimming around inside of me reminded me too much of the past. The past I wish didn't exist.

I never wanted to be one of those girls. The ones who did whatever they could to keep someone happy and to make them stay with them like I had just recently seen on TV or witnessed in the trades as the other girls desperately tried to please the men. The ones who went out of their way to be something they were not simply just to survive. I knew what it was like to survive, but I never tried to be something I wasn't while doing so. With Jared, I refused to be that as well.

I heard the slamming of the front door and the roar of the motorcycle as it was brought to life. The noise reminded me of the time we spent on it together just today. I had felt as if we were growing closer to one another, learning who the person hiding in the dark inside of us truly was. But now I see we really weren't.

"You're so dumb, Isabella..." I muttered into the air, frustrated I had allowed him pass my walls. He knew what I had been through yet he acted as he did? I tried to tell myself it had everything to do with being scared and afraid of the unknown, but in reality, I wasn't sure what it was.

Once again, I was stuck sitting here alone and in my thoughts because he walked away from me. Minutes ticked by, my stomach growling as a faint reminder of the fact that I hadn't even eaten dinner yet.

"If I told you that leaving was his fight or flight mechanism, would you believe me?" Bree's soft voice met my ears as I swung around toward the door of my bedroom. I must've been so wrapped up in what I was feeling, what Jared had caused me to feel that I failed to hear her come in.

"I would because he seems to fight against everything good in his life," I said truthfully. Her eyes sparkled with amusement as she smiled at me in understanding. We were both on the same page when it came to Jared.

"His past is lined with jagged rocks. He hasn't moved on from it and that's what is holding him back from finding the happiness he desperately is seeking." Bree walked into the room and took a seat on the edge of the bed. She eyed me cautiously as if she understood the hesitation that ate away at me.

"We all have a past that we never want to resurface. Mine is far worse than his I'm sure, but here I am going through the motions attempting to move on from it," I bit out. I was so angry he had allowed the past to douse the future in insecurities and pain. He was right about one thing—I did want to save him, but I also wanted more than that. I wanted to save us.

Bree's hand landed against my knee startling me. When I looked up into her dark eyes, I saw familiarity. It was the situation in general, the pain I had once endured. Maybe not in the same way, but she had endured something.

"Jared's past is a hard one. Many years ago he lost the only female he ever had in his life." She paused. "His mom was special to him. She died unexpectedly and it crushed him. Crushed our father, too. A lot of pain and time passed, and they found out I was the daughter our father had been looking for since he found out I existed. Through me, our dad found the little piece of happiness he had lost. I think there are times Jared harbors hard feelings toward me for giving our father something he couldn't. He looks around and sees everyone so happy while he still hasn't found his."

I understood what she was saying. It was like an itch that you got from poison ivy. If you scratched it over and over again, your skin would become irritated, and eventually, the itch would spread all over your body, causing irritation on every piece of your skin. Jared chose to wallow in his misery, to accept his pain as a burden until it tainted him completely from the inside out, spreading agony throughout him.

"He should be grateful for the family he has," I blurted out without thinking.

"He should be, but we all deal with pain in different ways. The easiest way to let something like that go is to push those who care about you away. It's easier to not feel when the pain is the worst because not feeling means it's not real. If you have no emotions toward it, you learn to numb it out."

One single tear fell from my eye. It was for Jared,

for the pain and hurting he was going through. He felt alone in his own world, and I knew what that felt like more than most.

"Don't cry for him. Don't let your tears be the symbol of forgiveness, sometimes people need to be pushed to their limits before they can learn to move on from the past. Every once in a while you have to push them off the emotional cliff so they can feel."

Her words echoed in my head, giving me the comfort I needed at that moment. Jared could say whatever he wanted to push me away, but at the end of the day, I knew what I felt inside of me for him. I knew, when he kissed me, he was just as lost in me as I was in him. I wasn't going to give in just yet. He was good at blocking people from getting too close, he even did it with his own family. Yet they didn't give up. If my feelings for him were as true as the words I spoke to him, then I couldn't either. I would push his boundaries and make him feel he couldn't walk away.

"How did you know he left?" I whispered softly to her, wondering if Jared had called her.

"He called Zerro. Told him he needed some time to breathe. Gia is with my dad, and I was already in the area, so I figured I would swing by."

"Well, thank you really, for coming by, for explaining the things that Jared fails to explain." As soon as the words left my lips, I realized just how messed up what I had said really was. I still had yet to explain to him what had happened to me. I knew he had some idea though as Alzerro was the reason I was free.

Bree laughed which in turn caused me to smile. "We all have a story that we have to tell as our own. He would've told you eventually. I just knew that right now I needed to tell you. Jared needs saving, and that's the bottom line. He needs someone to reach inside of him and pour her light and love into him. I know you have darkness inside of you still. I know this because, for a while, I had it in me. But the same way everyone saw my light even when I didn't, I see yours... Jared needs yours, Izzy."

Saving Jared. Those two words coinciding together in my mind, side by side, seemed as if they were impossible.

"I don't know if Jared can be saved," I spoke quietly, my fingers drifting over the soft blanket beneath me.

"We all can be saved. It's just more about when than *if*..."

I nodded my head in agreement knowing her words held the truth that could be reached if you had hope and faith—two things that had now become second nature to me.

I would have faith I could be the light for Jared—even in my own darkness, I would have enough hope for the both of us.

CHAPTER FIFTEEN

"SHE IS AS beautiful as she is smart. Fierce when she needs to be and quiet when she knows danger is lurking. She is an enigma and it is why she shall be yours." The salesman spoke with ease. He was a short man with a large midsection, telling me he lived a rather lavish lifestyle. His head was bald, and his eyes were dark and beady.

My eyes scanned the picture of the frail girl. Her eyes were dark and filled with fright. Her body was tiny, but you could tell she had a womanly body with curves created solely for hands to peruse. Her hair was long, dark, and curled.

She stood straight up, her chin held high as if she had a point to prove to someone. To most, it may have been a sign of disrespect, maybe even blatant anger. However, to me it was a sign of her worth. Even being treated as a piece of property, the simple gesture of holding her head high told me just how valuable she truly was.

"I want her," I growled, my hand gripping the photo with force. My cock was growing hard with images of taking her over and over again. She would be

INVINCIBLE

my little slut, my woman to do with as I pleased.

"Then she shall be yours, sir," the salesman replied. He sounded just as excited about the exchange as I did. That in turn made me smile. I gestured to Oliver and watched as he handed over the envelope of cash. Then I smiled even wider, knowing that sooner or later she would be mine. It was all in due time now.

"Boss, I have some news regarding Isabella." I lifted my eyes, pulling myself from the memory as I waved my hand, motioning for Wyatt to continue on with what he was saying. Wyatt had become one of my men about two months ago. His mother was in need of money when I plucked him from her, bringing him in as my own. Wyatt's hair had grown out a bit, the brown color looking ragged, his dark eyes bleeding into my own.

"She is being protected by the United States FBI. They have put her under witness protection." I narrowed my eyes at him. *Witness Protection?* Of course, they would enroll her in something like that as if it would make it less possible for me to find her.

"How do you know this is true?" I questioned, taking a drink of my whiskey. I watched his face grow white as snow as if he didn't want to tell me the lengths in which he had gone in order to find this tidbit of information.

"I have intel, They work closely with the agent who helped to rescue her. Said they were on the agent's special recovery team." I smiled. Money could change a good person into a bad person in five seconds.

"Anything else?" I asked another question, the whiskey in my glass swirling around in a hypnotizing way, drawing my attention to the caramel color that reminded me of her eyes in the picture I was given.

"We have yet to set eyes on her, but from what my intel has told me, she is being protected by a man. Adam's confirmation on location was correct. He is a driver for a company that does pickups and drop offs, only for the most important people in the state and has been spotted on French Island as he stated."

My fingers gripped the glass harder than expected thus causing the glass to shatter. Liquid dripped down my hand as glass pieces fell to the floor. *Another man was protecting her? From me, her owner?*

"Are you all right, sir?" Stephen rushed to my side as if I were a five-year-old unable to hold my own glass of water.

"Perfectly fine." I shoved him away as I got up from my seat in search of something to dry my hands with.

"What do you want to do next?" His question bounced around in my mind as I wiped the whiskey from my fingers. *What did I want to do next?* It was still too early for me to make my presence known, but I was also closer to her than I had ever been before. I had the choice to go in early without a well thought out plan and get what belonged to me, or I could act like the leader I was and find out everything I possibly could on the man who signed his death wish the moment he decided to be a hero.

"Gather some information. I need to know who this man is, and I want to know everything. From what he eats for breakfast to what color socks he has on. I will also need to know the exact company he works for, how many drives he goes on a week, even the routes he takes. And then once you've given me what my heart desires, I want to meet him. The man who dared to test Isabella's fate." I smiled sickly knowing that if I got the chance, I would beat the life from his body one drop of blood at a time.

"Meet him?" Wyatt's voice surrounded me, causing my jaw to tick. Was he questioning my motives? Or just me in general? With a flick of my wrist, I pulled my knife out, pushing it against his throat before he even had a chance to correct his mistake. He knew better than to question me. They all knew, yet they were all testing me lately it would seem. I stared into his eyes, thoroughly considering his death. I needed to show them just because Isabella had my mind all over the place, I still held their lives in the palm of my hand.

"What seems to be the issue, Wyatt? When I tell you to do something, you do it. Do you want to live, maybe continue to breathe?" I put pressure on the blade, causing it to press harder against his skin. I could see his skin breaking against the metal, a thin line of blood bubbling up over the blade.

"I didn't mean any harm, sir..." he stammered, his voice alone pissing me off even more.

"You didn't?" I leaned into him, my voice filled with disgust. Allowing him to walk away without harm being done to him would allow the other men to think they could question me whenever and however they pleased. That was a risk I was not willing to take. The whole reason they were here was because of me. My family had brought them into the United States. They owed me everything. Their lives most importantly. So when they fucked up, they paid in blood. That was the rule, their only option.

"I didn't, sir... You know I would never question you." Wyatt's eyes were begging me to extend my forgiveness, but there was no compassion in me to accept his plea. My body grew more and more alive with every passing second, waiting for another slip up so I could end his pathetic fucking life.

"That's funny because you already questioned me. So not only have you disobeyed my authority, you also lied straight to my face." Wyatt's breath came in heavy pants as I determined what was to be done with him.

"I should have your tongue cut off. Maybe then you would learn to never question me." I growled at him, squeezing his arm tightly as I jerked him over to the countertop of my bar. He was going to lose two fingers today. One for being Curious fucking George and another for lying to me. *My men knew better than this.*

"Sir..." Antonio called, but I paid no attention to him as I removed the knife from Wyatt's neck. Whatever he had to say to me would have to wait. I pushed Wyatt down so that the top half of his body was flushed against the smooth surface, his hand laid out in front of me. It was a shame to have to do this to him, I thought briefly as I held the blade up, watching it gleam in the light. Then I gripped his wrist hard, pushing it harder against the countertop. Wyatt's eyes continued to silently plead with me, but there was no turning back now. I had already taken my knife out and it was hungry for more blood.

"This is your offering to me for your transgressions. Let this be a lesson to you." I smiled just as I brought the blade down on his thumb and pointer finger. His agony filled scream filled the air as the blade cut through his skin and bone with ease. Blood dripped from the blade as I lifted it up, crimson droplets falling on the surface. Wyatt yanked his hand from the table, hysterical screams falling from his lips.

"Remove him and send Stephen to clean this

INVINCIBLE

mess," I told Antonio, taking a seat back at my desk in the middle of my office. I held the blade in my hand, completely captivated by the blood.

More blood would be shed.

People would die and it would all be at my hands.

I was the new king of the mafia.

CHAPTER SIXTEEN

Jared

THE LIGHTS INSIDE the bar blinded me, reminding me more and more why I shouldn't be drinking, I told myself as I brought the beer to my lips. Her dark locks of hair in my mind. Her eyes were full of pleasure as she sank her teeth into her bottom lip.

Shaking my head, I forced the image of her away. What was the point of leaving and coming here if I had continued to think about her after I was gone? She was fucking with my head, crawling under my skin, and embedding herself deep inside of me.

"Another?" The blonde behind the bar asked, signaling toward my beer. I tipped my chin up at her letting her know I would, in fact, take another.

"What the fuck is up with you?" I rolled my eyes. I knew that voice and I knew what it brought. *A fucking headache.*

"Nothing is up with me. I'm simply having a beer after a long, strenuous day of work." Alzerro took the seat next to me, a beer sitting in front of him before I could turn to face him. One look at him told me he needed a drink more than I did. His hair was a mess, his eyes creased in worry.

He laughed low, his voice darker than usual. "You working? Really? I have yet to see a day where you were actually working." I clenched my fist reminding myself of how rude it truly was to punch your best friend slash brother-in-law in the face, even if he did deserve it. *Once an asshole, always an asshole.*

"Isabella is a lot more work than you told me she would be." I cursed myself the moment the words left my mouth. I had all but opened the door to a conversation about Isabella and me. Even more, I had opened up the chance to discuss my feelings. He tipped his beer back, a smile curving around the top of the bottle.

"Doesn't matter what kind of woman they are. A woman, in general, is more work than just some easy lay." Of course, he was speaking from experience. He was married to my sister after all.

"At least Bree isn't being chased by the Russian Mafia and forced to live with a man who is unstable, and unavailable in every emotional sense." Fuck! I had to be drinking something stronger than beer. There was no way I was having a deep conversation so open and freely with him.

"I think you have forgotten about the past. If I'm not mistaken, Bree once found herself in the home of a Mafia King with no way out." He nudged my shoulder causing me to smile without cause.

"Oh, no. I remember the big ole mean Mafia King you used to be. That's beside the point though. Isabella deserves better living conditions." There was no way I was going to tell him she was causing me to feel things—things I had never felt in my life. That she was slowly worming her way into my mind and body, and eventually, she would end up in my soul, too. I could feel myself grow weaker for her touch every single day.

"I know the last three years I have been hard on you, wanting you to be the person I grew up with, so much so that every time I called or came over, I ended up telling you to get your shit together instead of giving you actual advice. But I want to tell you something, something that has changed how I look at things over the years. Something that turned me from that person, the Mafia King, who didn't give two fucks who's blood he spilled, into just Alzerro King." I wanted to roll my eyes and tell him to shut up, but instead, I stopped myself wondering what kind of advice he wanted to give me. Then he opened his mouth and something I had never heard came out.

"Fear is only what you make of it. What you fear isn't really something you're scared of, but something you think you are afraid of. Imagine everything you have ever wanted in your life is on the other side of that fear... What are you going to do to get to it? Conquer that fear or risk the chance of losing everything—of losing *her*?" My eyes grew wide, the air in my chest evaporated, and my heartbeat accelerated. I could feel the desire to flee taking over.

"Don't even think about it." His hand landed heavily on my shoulder, keeping me in place. *Grounding me.*

"I can't be at risk of losing something that was never mine," I growled. Being alone was always for the best when it came to me. It was easier to hide the pain than to face it head on.

INVINCIBLE

"She was yours the moment I told you to protect her. I saw the look in your eyes, Jared. Lie to yourself, to her, but you can't lie to me because I see in you what I once felt within myself. The desire to be healed. I don't know what you're battling deep down inside of yourself, but I promise you if you open yourself up, she'll be the one to heal you." Misery, suffering, and rage were what I was battling deep within me. I was broken, the pain killing me slowly.

"I don't want your advice. I don't want to be told how to love someone. I just want to be left the fuck alone." I threw a twenty down on the bar and got my keys out of my pocket. Being home with Isabella might cause a thousand and one emotions to flow through me, but listening to Zerro talk about ways to heal my nonexistent heart was pissing me off far more than that.

"You're welcome." He threw the remark over his shoulder as I headed toward the bar entrance. Forcing myself outside and away from him, I drank in the night, allowing deep breaths of air to filter into my lungs. My head was a mess, my body begging me to give it things it desired.

Jumping on my bike, I started it and revved the engine allowing the noise to fill me. *You got this. You know what's best for you, not anyone else.* Zooming off like a bat out of hell, I headed home weaving in and out of traffic as I went. Five minutes later, I pulled into my driveway. All the lights in the house were off and there was no music blaring from inside like last time. This time, there was only quietness and peace, both things settling deep into my bones.

I cut the engine and then hopped off my bike, walking to the front door. My hand gripped the metal door handle tightly. It was cold and solid, bringing me back to the present. I reached in my pocket, removing my key and unlocking the door. With a twist of the knob, I entered the house only to discover it looked as if no one was here. My heart ached, a twisting feeling growing in my belly. *What if she left?*

Something told me there would be no coming back from that. I might have been trying to push her away, to make her see I had nothing to offer, but pushing her as far as making her leave was never my intention. Did I push her too far this time? The twisting in my stomach grew more and more as I walked around the house. Nothing was out of place, yet the walls held an alarming eerie quietness to them.

Whipping my jacket off, I headed toward her room, my booted feet heavy against the wood floor. *I have to know,* I thought as I came to a halt at her door. It was slightly opened, but no sounds of peaceful slumber could be heard through it.

Lifting my hand unsteadily, I pushed it open the rest of the way. My eyes landing on her empty bed. It was made, sheets pulled up, and it looked as if no one had even attempted to lay in it.

"Fuck!" I said loudly, slamming my fist into the wall. *Fuck.* Had I really pushed the only good thing to happen in my life away? My feet pounded back down the hallway toward my bedroom. Rage surged through my veins as I all but knocked the bedroom door open, barely noticing the sleeping form in my bed. The blankets were pulled up to her shoulders and she was curled into herself.

She stirred slightly, and I cursed myself for being such a reckless asshole. I had failed to check the entire house before slamming shit around, before making a rash decision to do something stupid. Sitting on the edge of the bed, I removed my boots and clothes. Once just in my boxers, I pulled the covers back, my cock growing hard with every slip of the fabric off her skin. My eyes lingered on her bare back and then down where I found a shapely ass that was, in fact, naked. *Fucking Christ.*

I gripped my hair hard. She was playing games with me—fucking with my head and messing with my heart. This was no longer the game of who could push who harder, no—now we're on the verge of dangerous territory. She wanted to give herself to me, or at least it seemed that way. Instead of crawling into bed with her and sliding between her warm thighs, I walked to the other side of the bed, shaking her softly. Her eyes popped open immediately, they, of course, were heavy with sleep, but there was something more underneath. The look was smoldering, devouring even as if she would do whatever she could to get a taste of me.

I was done denying my body what it wanted most when it came to her. She wanted to play with fire. I smiled to myself as the devil himself.

Then she best be ready to get burnt.

CHAPTER SEVENTEEN

Isabella

MY EYES POPPED open as a hand rubbed against my shoulder. I wanted to moan but pushed the desire away. Darkness shadowed the room, and as my eyes adjusted to the light, I realized Jared was standing before me. He was naked, his boxers gone, his cock pointing straight at me.

"You have been pushing your luck, Isabella. Pushing me mentally, emotionally, and now physically." He spoke the words with force as if he were on edge. I wanted to smile, simply because I knew this would be the last straw for him. *He would break at the will of my touch.*

His finger skimmed over my skin, and I heaved a breath in as I lay there exposing myself to his wickedness.

Jared stared at me for a few long moments, his eyes gliding up and down my body numerous times. I felt like he was taking a mental picture of me with every swipe of his eyes.

"You're much more beautiful than I had ever thought you would be." His voice was deep, sending a tremble through my entire body.

"I want you. I don't want to fight this anymore." My words were final. I knew I would never take them back because I saw something inside of him I felt every day inside of myself. I might not love Jared right now, but I cared deeply for him and given the opportunity, I could love him one day. Possibly, if we both allowed ourselves to give and accept that love.

His eyes darkened, his fists clenching and unclenching. He was fighting it, fighting me.

Sitting up, I pushed myself off the mattress and crawled to the edge of the bed on my hands and knees. His cock was jutting forward, stiff and ready for me causing my core to pulsate with dark desires.

"So what's your move?" he asked, his cockiness dripping off him in waves. I had never willingly bared myself before, yet my confidence was through the roof.

"Bringing you to your knees." I smiled gripping his thickness in my hand. My tongue flicked out wetting my lips. The hardness of it frightened me but did nothing to inhibit me from moving forward. To have him inside of me thrusting, it fueled my need, turning it into an unbridled passion.

"No…" He growled but made no move to pull away. I waited a moment and then another before leaning in closer and licking the tip. It was smooth like velvet, soft against my tongue. Maintaining my grip, I sucked him in and out of my mouth slowly, only taking what I could handle. After all, I was no pro at this.

"Fuck…" The raspiness of his voice vibrated through me as I smiled against his cock. Before I could take him back in, it was as if something in him snapped. In a blink of an eye, I was pinned to the mattress on my stomach while my hips were being gripped and pulled to the edge of the bed.

"I have thought about eating the fuck out of this pussy since the first day I met you. I wondered if it would glisten just for me..." he trailed off as his finger glided up my inner thigh, stopping at my entrance briefly before entering me slowly. I could feel his warm breath against my bare flesh and then he was burying his face into my center as he sucked my clit into his mouth.

"Ahhh..." The moan slipped past my lips with ease, my body filling with emotions I had never felt before. Every touch of his lips and flick of his tongue against me, each suck and push of his finger heated me from the inside out with a tingling sensation that was building deep within me.

"Come. Come for me." His voice was animalistic giving me the last push I needed to fall off that cliff. A shiver ran through my body as an array of lights formed behind my lids. I felt as if I could feel everything at a heightened rate, my body still exploding as Jared's lips slid against the skin on my back.

"I've tried fighting it. Tried pushing you away but I can't anymore. I can't keep fighting against whatever this is that is taking place between us. Every time I say no, the universe finds a way to push us back together..." I understood his emotions and it was at that moment I realized I didn't want to save him. It had never really been about saving. It was about making him whole again, about picking up those lingering pieces of heart and putting them back together, about opening up those old wounds and burying myself deep within them.

I was being carried away by my own emotions, feelings swarming at every angle.

"I want you," I whispered, pushing back against him. I didn't care that it was my first time. All my inhibitions were running wild. All I cared about was I was here at this moment with Jared and it would be him bringing me pleasure with each slam of his hips on my own.

"Good," he stated, his voice coming out wicked. "I didn't ever want you to see this side of me." He flipped me over so I was on my back in the center of the mattress. Then he leaned over me, the muscles of his body taut and tight as they strained against his flesh.

"I want to see all the different sides of you, the dark, the light, the sides you never want to show people. I want, too," I confessed, not realizing I had done so out loud until he spoke again.

"We'll see if you still feel that way and want to stay after I'm done with you." There was a warning to his words as if he expected me to walk away after all of this was said and done. I smiled letting him know his scare tactic hadn't worked. I still wanted him, if not more now than before.

I watched intently as he reached over to the nightstand that sat by the side of the bed. I could hear him rummaging around but stayed still, the anticipation of the unknown causing worries to run rampant through my mind.

"Lift your hands and place them on the bed railing." I did as I was told, his tone causing me to shiver. Jared was unable to control what we felt for one another. He commanding me right now was his way of regaining that control back. A red rope appeared in his hands and my stomach fell. *Was he going to tie me up?*

"Don't look at me like I'm going to hurt you. I would never hurt you," he whispered into my ear wrapping the silk around my wrists and securing me against the bars. Every rub of the fabric against my skin heightened my senses as the softness of it mixed with the hardness of Jared rubbed across my chest and belly.

"Please..." I begged and pleaded, my eyes bleeding into his. His fingers trailed down my chest and between my breasts, his fingers grazing my nipples as he passed them. He was taking his sweet time with me, savoring every touch as if it would be his last.

"Doing this..." His hands gripped my thighs as he centered himself at my entrance, "changes nothing between us." I could feel him pressing against me and my insides quivered in every way possible. I didn't care about the words he was saying because I knew they weren't true. He was trying to protect himself, and I would let him think as he did for a short time.

"Do you understand?" His words were tense, and I shook my head yes, all while knowing this changed everything. Sex changed everything for me.

With his hands on my hips and his eyes locked on mine, he entered me as slow as humanly possible. I watched his body quiver with restraint as he tried to control himself.

Pain filled my belly, causing my hands to lock up and my body to tremble uncontrollably. Without thought, I squeezed my legs together as if I could make the pain go away while clamping my mouth to close in hopes no sounds would leave my lips.

"You didn't tell me..." He growled, pulling out and pushing back into me as tenderly as possible. The push caused more pain to radiate throughout my limbs, causing the softest whimper to fill the air. Unable to handle the sting of him pushing past my barrier and the emotions surging through me, I turned my face away from him. Shame was riddling me, pushing the happiness away. His hand reached up, cupping my cheek so I had no other choice but to look at him.

"You should've told me." He pulled out and re-entered me slowly, causing a whimper to escape my lips. His mouth descended downwards, swallowing my moans as his own. In that kiss, there was so much passion, so many secrets, so much love, yet so much hurt. In that kiss, I had every answer I ever needed. Jared might have been struggling with processing his feelings for me, but all I needed was this. When he kissed me, it wasn't he kissing my lips, but him leaving an indent upon my soul.

With soft and subtle strokes, the pain subsided and in its place pleasure bloomed. His hands painted a picture against my skin that only we could understand. His lips devoured me, speaking to me without a single word. His body spoke the things he could never say.

My panting breaths mixed with his groans filled the air, causing my libido to go through the roof. Every slick inch of him could be felt in my womb. Our bodies mingled together, the slaps of our skin hitting one another were a song of pure pleasure.

He mended the broken pieces of me while I held us together like glue.

"Angel…." he said, placing a feather light kiss against my forehead. I could feel him pulsing inside of me and then a drop of wetness fell from his eye landing against my skin. In that one drop was his will to hold onto the past—he was letting it go.

As he came, he filled me with happiness, love—but

most of all self-worth. I may have been promised to another man, bought and traded against my will, but I would never regret meeting Jared.

"Thank you," I said aloud, wanting him to know him taking this part of me made me eternally grateful. He had no idea the power he held over me.

"No. It's I who is grateful. You pushed me to my limit. Forced me to feel again and for that I am forever grateful." I smiled just as he pulled out of me and rolled over to lie down beside me. He tucked me into his chest with his palm placed against my skin. The warmth of his flesh against mine calmed my roaring emotions.

His arms trembled around me as he held us together, binding us as one being. Jared was the one thing I had always wanted. He was that thing on the other side of my fear. He gave me that chance to open up, to be loved and cared for, and I in turn, took his hate and wove it into a love story so deep and true.

He had imprinted himself upon my heart.

CHAPTER EIGHTEEN

MEMORIES FROM JUST hours ago filtered into my mind, the force of them wrapping me in a blanket of warmth. Her moans and pants for more and the sweet nothings that fell from her plump lips reminded me of how much I didn't deserve her, but how much I craved her. Being with her was like heaven and even if I knew I would be sinning a thousand times over by being with someone as great as she was, I would still do it.

She had a way of making my chest swell with feelings I had never felt in my entire life. She was attempting to heal old wounds, ones that had formed and scabbed over, again and again until a scar formed. She wanted to be my saving grace, and looking at her right now, I knew I would let her. She would be the person to piece me back together.

I glanced down at her sleeping form, her hair a wild disoriented mess of darkness, similar to my soul. I pushed some strands away from her face, tracing the contours of it with my finger, my nose gliding against the side of her cheek. Taking a deep whiff, I could smell my scent covering her body. I had claimed her. I had made her mine.

INVINCIBLE

Pulling away, I continued to stare, but without touching her. She was an enigma, a woman who had been taken against her will and forced into a life she neither wanted nor understood. She was fearless, diving into the bastard I claimed myself to be. Ready to take on the world, if only to see a smile shine from my face.

She deserved more, better.

The thought entered my mind before I could push it away. I knew the honesty of the thought even if I refused to admit it out loud. My heart wanted her, to keep her as my own. My mind told me I was far too flawed, broken, and undeserving of someone as her. There were jagged pieces from my past that had the potential of cutting anyone who got too close.

She stirred awake, her eyes blinking open. The sun had just started to rise, and I wanted to give her a chance to rest, as there would be no controlling myself around her now. One taste of her would never be enough to extinguish the cravings she caused within me.

"Good morning," she moaned, stretching in such a way that had my eyes gliding over every single piece of uncovered flesh.

"Morning." I smiled, placing a kiss against her lips.

The air between us was a draft as if something was in the way. Her nose scrunched up, and lines of frustration started to form on her face.

"What's a matter?" Concerned she may have actually realized just exactly what kind of douchebag I was.

Isabella hesitated for a moment, her mouth opening, and then slamming closed. She chewed on her lip nervously before speaking. "It's just that last night you said this doesn't change anything." She seemed to be watching me, waiting for me to say something to her.

"I lied to you when I said it wouldn't because it does. It changes everything. You might be able to walk away, you might be able to wash away my memory, but in my mind, you will always be the most perfect person I have ever had."

The frown that marred her lips made me feel like the world's biggest jackass for saying such a thing last night. I knew the moment my cock pressed into her everything had changed. I was just trying to convince myself it hadn't. As I said, my mind knew the truth, but my heart still wanted her, and so I took without disregard.

"Isabella…" I let her name roll off my tongue. This time when I said it, I saw her and not the memory of my mother.

"The moment you walked through the front door was the moment everything in my life changed. It wasn't just about unraveling you and becoming one with you. I was on my knees, and melting in your hands the moment my eyes landed on you." My words lingered in the air between us, and before I could allow her to say anything, I needed to finish.

"I was half a man then, incapable of loving, or so I thought. You changed me, you molded the broken pieces together, you healed the scars that covered my heart, and you held me together when I felt as if I was falling helplessly into the deep end." My words were spoken straight from the heart. The feelings that accompanied them had never been more real. Call me a sap ass, but I was falling in love, and I didn't even care that there was a chance I could be hurt again. There came a time when you had to let the past stop defining your future.

INVINCIBLE

"I..." She seemed flabbergasted as if she wasn't even sure what she wanted to say. "I know that sex can change things between people..." She trailed off, but I lost track of her words. My eyes focused in on her, my heart beating out of my chest as I reached out to her. She was worried for legit reasons, but she wasn't aware of the power she held.

"You rescued me from myself. In a way, you became my anchor. So though I might have fought against your desires to be anything more than what we were in the past, I always knew it was you my heart wanted." I gripped her face, bringing it closer to my own. The closeness of her body was causing my cock to grow stiff again. Would I ever get enough of her? She was intoxicating, overwhelming me with every turn.

"Jared..." She said my name in a throaty moan. I was just about to flip her over and have my way with her when my phone blared from the nightstand, the ringtone one I used strictly for work.

"Fuck. Hold on a sec." I placed a kiss on her cheek and untangled myself from her body, missing the heat of her skin immediately. Picking up the phone, I hit the answer key and waited for my boss to speak.

"Jared."

"Xavier." I greeted him in the same tone he did me.

"We have a job for you. I need you to pick up a man in Shillington and bring him here to French Island." I wanted to sigh into the phone. Of course, work would rain on my fucking parade. And just when I found the one woman who I would gladly stay in bed with all day.

"Time and price," I asked as I got up out of bed, shucking on a pair of pants as I went. I could hear Izzy's protests, so I shot her a wink over my shoulder. I hated

I had to work, but I knew this was important. If Xavier was contacting me by phone, it meant someone had asked specifically for me as a driver.

"Thirty minutes from now. Two grand. Didn't say what he needed just asked for you." Xavier's voice was firm, as it always was.

"All right, text me the details. I'll let you know when I have him picked up." I hung up the phone throwing it onto the bed. Izzy's eyes were drilling holes into me as I moved around the room attempting to find a shirt. I could hear her moan, and when I looked over, I caught sight of her touching herself. She was spread eagle on the bed, her knees drawn up at an angle that showed me her soaking pussy.

"I wish it was you doing this..." she trailed off, inserting one finger and then another into her pussy. The room grew hotter with every stroke she made. Without hesitation, my pants hit the floor and I fisted my cock in my hand.

"Fuck that sweet pussy..." I urged, kneeling on the edge of the bed as her eyes drifted closed and her pace upped. The grip I had on my cock tightened as I stroked it forcefully.

"Ahhhh..." I could tell she was almost at her peak, so I went faster.

"Imagine my cock deep inside of you, drilling into you at a relentless pace, making every inch of you mine from the inside out..." My voice was now a growl as my own release lingered right on the surface.

"Fuck..." I heard her sweet little mouth say as her motions became jerky and her knees began to collapse. We kept our eyes trained on one another as I jerked my release onto her body. I smiled down at her as she gave me a sleepy grin. I have never been so fucking turned on in my life.

I cleared my throat. "Get you and that beautiful ass out of this bed and jump in the shower with me. You're coming with me to work." She smiled and moved from the bed slowly as if she didn't want to move at all. We showered quietly washing each other—bodies and hair. Then I got dressed and made us coffee placing it in to-go cups. We hadn't really spoken while showering or getting dressed, and honestly, that was fine with me. My body had said everything it needed to say.

As we made our way out into the garage and then into the Tahoe, she asked, "Who are you picking up?"

"I don't know. I'm never given a name or what they do for a living. I simply take them. Sometimes they might request for me to pick up a package for them or drop one off," I said as we pulled out of the garage, down the driveway and onto the road. Heading toward the destination Xavier had sent me, I noticed the GPS coordinates were sending me to a warehouse in the business district.

"Do you like doing this?" She shot me another question, her hand reaching over the center console and landing against my knee. Her touch was causing my blood to boil. The need to ravish her was dangerously close.

"Yes, I suppose I do. I never really had time not to like it. Even my dad used to be a driver for Alzerro King's dad actually. He would take me on drives sometimes and that was how I met Zerro. We were childhood friends growing up, and when I got older, I took over for my dad as he did for his." I ignored her touch, which was causing my cock to rise in my pants.

"How did you meet him?" Her hand moved closer to my zipper. This woman was about to find out just how not under control I truly was.

"Alzerro used to be part of the mafia. He ran all of French Island and the surrounding areas. He was a cold-blooded killer who was hell bent on making others pay for the destruction that had happened in his life." Her hand stopped moving as the car filled with tension.

"He killed people?" she asked. I didn't want to tell her about the past, about the man he used to be, but she had every right to know how I came to know him. About my past. If I wanted to move forward, I needed to let go of the past, and opening up to her was the first step.

"Yes. He killed a lot of people. Most deserved it, but some didn't. Just like myself—he wasn't in a good place in his life. Then he met Bree and everything kind of changed." Thinking back on it, Alzerro's change was similar to my own. He had lost his mother and needed to find vengeance for her. I had lost my mother and the absence of her had caused a coldness to settle over me. I thought finding out Bree was my sister would help. I thought seeing my dad the happiest he has ever been would change things, but the truth was nothing could cover up the ice that had settled around my heart if I didn't let anyone in.

"You're a good person, Jared. You were just lost, hurting, and alone. Everyone does weird things when they feel as if the world is slipping from their hands. " Her hand gripped my thigh hard, trying to grab my attention. The fact that she understood made my heart rate rise. She knew everything I had failed to tell others, even her. She paid better attention than I had ever expected her to.

"Just remember that when times get hard and the darkness starts to encompass me. I'm not an easy person to be around at my best, let alone my worst," I warned. *I didn't want to push her away, but I wanted her to know what she was getting herself into,* I thought as I pulled into the factory parking lot, noticing just how vacant the place was.

"I'll remember and I'll be the person to bring you out of it. You just remember that," she whispered just as a man in a black suit started walking toward the car. His hair was slicked back, his chin held high and his eyes dialed in on the car. Each of his steps held a purpose as if it were bringing him one step closer to something he was desperately seeking. Her eyes lifted toward the man, and I saw the fear resonate with them.

"It's going to be okay." I soothed her, knowing how meeting new people had to be a shock to her. What she had gone through to get where she was wasn't an easy feat.

"Okay," she said simply, smiling. It was in that smile I knew she had lied to me. It wasn't going to be okay. It was going to be far from okay. I just didn't realize it right then.

CHAPTER NINETEEN

I WANTED TO laugh loudly and uncontrollably at the man behind the wheel. *This was him? The hero of the story?* The man housing my soon to be wife, my queen, my fucking pet. I could feel the anger in me waiting to be unleashed. All it would take was a simple snap of the neck or a shot to the back of his head delivered by me. Yet as I took my seat, I knew I couldn't do it.

I wouldn't because I wanted him to suffer, to know who it was that was making him bleed. As I sunk further into the leather, I allowed my eyes to linger over them, eventually stopping and narrowing on the back of *her* head. I could see her hair and the slope of her neck. It was far darker than I remember it being. I couldn't see her face, but from the movements she was making, I could tell she knew something was wrong. Her sixth sense telling her danger lay within touching distance.

My teeth ground together as the man sitting next to her placed his hand on hers. That one movement almost made me change my mind.

"It's okay," I heard him whisper to her. He had no idea just how wrong he truly was. Nothing would be okay until her life was put in my hands. He was giving her false hope, teaching her the unknown was okay. She was foolish to believe him if she did.

"Thank you for coming on such short notice," I interrupted, not wanting them to continue on with their intimate conversation. *They were disgusting.*

His eyes flashed to mine in the rearview mirror. He was sizing me up and down, and I could see the panic forming in his head. He had every reason to be afraid.

"Of course." He cleared his throat. I continued to stare at Isabella in the front seat afraid if I looked away, she would disappear. Pulling my phone out, I knew I needed to make a phone call to my men. The drive I had scheduled was only a half hour long, long enough for me to be able to verify it was her. Having done so, I could now put my plan into motion.

"French Island is a nice place, yes?" I asked, wanting to make light conversation. It was best for people to not see you as an enemy. That way they never saw the attack coming, they never would expect you to place a bullet in the back of their head.

"Yes. Great schools, a nice small community." Again, he was telling me about shit I couldn't care less about, yet I played along as if I had known him the entire time.

"Have you two lived here long? My poor manners, assuming she is your special someone in your life."

Silence met my ears as I watched Isabella fidget in her seat. She couldn't have realized how close to danger she truly was.

"Uh, yeah. I have lived here my whole life. Isabella is my…" He seemed to linger on the word that he wanted to say. "Girlfriend, we just started dating so, yeah, she's my special someone…" He finally got the words out, but behind them was a feeling that told me he was unsure. His eyes flickered from the road and then back to her.

"What a beautiful woman she is." I complimented her just to get a rouse out of him. I wanted to do anything I could do to make him squirm in his skin. I wanted him weak, vulnerable.

"Yes, very beautiful." He seemed tickled pink with love. Again, I felt myself on the verge of vomiting—that or revealing who I was just so I could make him suffer. My phone rang right on cue, as it should've—my men knew that if they failed to follow orders given that they would lose something.

"Sir." Antonio's voice sounded in my ears.

"Его она," I spoke in Russian.

"Confirmation is in order, moving to the next step in our plan." He repeated the words that needed to be said back to me before hanging up. I pressed the end key on my phone, placing my hands on my lap.

Then I sat back and watched.

Their lives would be ending soon. Hers because she would no longer have freedom, and his for touching something that was mine.

CHAPTER TWENTY

Isabella

EVERYTHING ABOUT TODAY felt off, at least from the moment we pulled into the parking lot of that abandoned parking lot. The air around me filled with tension and danger. The man in the backseat oozed money—his suit, even his smell. He reminded me of the man Jared had said Alzerro was before he found Bree, not just that, but he reminded me of everything I wanted to distance myself from. I fidgeted with my hands nervously, feeling as if the man in the back seat was staring straight through to my heart as if he could see the fear within me.

Jared held my hand, attempting to soothe me. It worked until it came time to drop the man off. It was when Jared removed his hand from mine the fear slithered its way back into me. I felt naked and cold without him.

I could feel the man in the back seat glaring at me,

his eyes practically burning my skin. I was rooted in place while I waited the minuscule amount of seconds it took Jared to get to his door and let him out. The entire three seconds I felt he had something he wanted to say—as if there were unsaid words floating between the two of us.

"Thank you," he said to Jared. I didn't miss the fact he had spoken Russian in the backseat. I knew better than to dismiss something that big. When Jared got back in the car, I tried to seem unaffected by the man's presence but the thing was, I couldn't shake it.

"I thought I could grill out tonight. We could sit on the porch swing and eat dinner together." I could feel Jared's hand on my own but felt disconnected from him. I was putting up a wall, shielding myself from the destruction I felt was going to take place soon.

"That…" I paused. "That sounds great." I faked a smile, not wanting him to know just how alone I was truly feeling.

He was worried about me. I could see it on his face, yet he failed to let it hinder him. Instead, he pushed it away just as I gripped his hand in mine. I didn't need him asking more questions or wanting to delve deeper into things. I knew I was a hypocrite for doing this, for failing to tell him what my instincts were telling me, but I needed to protect him.

He had finally opened up to someone, and there was no way in hell I would take that away from him. As we drove back to the house, I searched my mind for a memory, a picture, anything to tell me who the man was. Then something hit me. It could've been the smell that still lingered in the car or the way his voice sounded in Russian as I replayed it over and over again in my mind. The repeating forced a memory to come forward.

"Which one is mine?" a male voice asked. I didn't move. I knew better. I had heard many of the other girls beat for moving.

"This one right here." One of the men gripped my arm pulling me up onto my unsteady legs. It had been days since they removed the bag from my head. They only ever removed it when we ate. One girl told me it was easier for the men if they didn't have to see our faces all the time.

"She is so tiny," the man commented. I could feel his hand on my waist, his fingers lingering on my skin. His scent engulfed me, reminding me of high-end collagen. He had money—that much was true.

"Most of them are, sir. We buy them as is and due to certain circumstances, we cannot offer them everything needed. Sometimes we have to discipline them. As you can see, some of them have flesh wounds and bruises. It comes with the territory." I had seen death many times over since I was sold. They didn't care if we lived or died. Only the ones worth a pretty penny survived.

I could feel the air around me grow tense. It was thickening making it harder to breathe. I stood very still, afraid if I moved even an inch, I would be backhanded, and maybe even have my chance at freedom taken from me.

"You're to treat her with respect. She is more expensive than any of the others you're holding. I paid far more than anyone else," the man growled. There was violence in his voice, and it consumed me.

"Yes... yes, sir," the man stuttered over his words as if he were afraid of my soon to be owner, which made me wonder if I should be, as well.

"Good. I want no ill harm to come to her, and if I find out that any has, blood will be shed in her honor." There was no lightheartedness to his words. He cupped my cheek and whispered near my ear, his breath fresh and sweet.

"Дитя, ты в порядке с предприятием." I didn't know what he had said, but I did know it did very little to soothe me. I knew better than to hope the place I would be taken to would be much better than this one.

"Protect her at all cost. Otherwise, it's your life that will be taken." Those were the last words he had said before his footsteps sounded off in the distance.

"Izzy…" Jared called my name. His hand was gripping mine as if he wanted to keep me here with him forever. It was as if he knew and understood I was going to drift far away.

"Yes?" I turned to him. The memory had felt so real—as if I was truly there again enduring the pains of my past.

"Are you okay? You seemed lost in thought for a second there." It was then I noticed we were parked in his driveway. His other hand lifted up, cupping my cheek just as the man in my memory had.

"Everything is okay now, no one can hurt you. I promise you that. I would die before I let anything happen to you." What Jared was saying was supposed to comfort me, talk me off that cliff of insecurity, but it didn't. I knew what the future held. I could feel it in my bones. The uncertainty of it all.

"I know, and thank you for that." I placed a kiss on his lips, wanting him to know although my mind was elsewhere, he impacted me in so many ways, ways words would never be able to describe.

"You have no idea how much you have changed me for the better." His words weighed heavily on my mind as we got out of the car and headed into the house. I took small steps, knowing closing the front door of the house would be when I needed to clear my mind. I didn't want to worry Jared any more than he already was. Alzerro had him protecting me, but he also had the stuff of his own going on.

Once inside, Jared found himself searching the fridge for food to make for dinner. I couldn't think of anything else but him as I stared, watching his every move.

"Keep staring at me like that and I'll bend you right over this island." He smirked, looking up from the veggies he had grabbed out of the fridge. I smiled innocently, pulling the top of my dress down to expose my bra covered breasts. As I rounded the island, I caught the sound of the knife hitting the counter and Jared's footsteps right behind me. I stood very still as his hand worked its way from my shoulder down to the top of my breast.

"Do you want to be fucked on this counter?" he asked curiously, his mouth against my neck. His lips were causing my mind to drift away, and the current was about to take me out to sea.

Instead of answering him, I pulled the side of my dress up revealing the secret I hadn't told him about yet. His other hand slid up my thigh giving way to what it was I was hiding. With a light push, I landed against the countertop, my breasts reacting to the coldness of the marble beneath me.

"No panties?" he said shocked, his finger slipping in between my folds. I released a sigh from my throat as the pleasure overwhelmed me.

"I did it for you," I moaned as he hovered over me, his lips sucking on my earlobe. My eyes drifted closed just as his finger slipped into me. I was sore from the night before, but the pleasure seemed to override the pain as he slowly slipped in and out of me.

INVINCIBLE

"You're far more than I ever deserved, far more than I ever needed." He was speaking to my heart taking me closer and closer to the finish line with every push of his thick digit inside of me.

"Come for me," he growled into my ear, his teeth sinking into my sensitive flesh once again. His hand cupped my sex as his free hand lifted one of my legs off the ground while he continued to pump in and out of me. The intensity of his movements with the raspy panting of his voice caused my core to clench. My legs tingled and my back arched as pleasure moved through me.

"So fucking beautiful. You're soaked for me. Now I can fuck you like I've wanted to all day long." He grunted as he undid his pants. I could hear the clanking of his belt as it fell to the floor. I was ready for him, ready to be possessed.

"Give me every last inch of you," I whimpered, feeling deep inside of me that this might be our last time together, and if that was so, I wanted to remember this moment for the rest of my life.

His cock pressed against my entrance as he lifted me, pushing me further onto the counter causing the items upon it to fall to the floor, without a care in the world.

"You're mine," he hissed out, his hand landing heavily on the back of my neck as he pressed my front down and pulled my ass up. I sighed as he slammed into me without warning. His balls slapping against my clit with so much intensity, I almost came just from the friction alone.

"It will always be you," I spoke, my breath hot against my skin as I tried to muffle my screams. His nails bit into my flesh as if he understood the finality that this last session had between us.

"Every time you move, I want you to feel me. Every time you finger yourself, I want you to think about my cock deep inside of you." His hips gyrated as my eyes rolled to the back of my head.

"I'm going to come," I screamed. It was then I felt him pull out of me, the absence of him making me grow cold.

"No. You come when I say you can." I felt his cock slip back into me, only to be pulled back out and slipped in between my ass cheeks.

"Please..." I begged as I tried to dig my nails into the counter. It was the singular beg that pushed him over the edge allowing me to have what he was giving me.

His hands gripped my flesh hard as he pushed me harder to the edge of the counter. I could feel his cock, but whimpered as it slipped away from my entrance.

"You want to come, you're going to have to ride me," he growled, placing his cock at my entrance. That was the only warning I needed. I slammed myself back into him, our flesh slapping against one another's echoing throughout the house.

"Ride it, baby..." Jared's voice turned dark as his hand pulled my hair tightly against my scalp. It was with that pleasure and pain that I came. My pussy clenched around him like a vice as I rode out each wave of pleasure. The waves grew bigger and bigger as he took over pumping into me until there was nothing left of the two of us.

It was at that moment I realized I loved him and I wanted a future with him—but it was all too late.

Death was coming for us.

CHAPTER TWENTY-ONE

Jared

I COULDN'T GET enough of her. The way her eyes drifted closed when she came all over my cock. The darkness in them when she bit her lip and looked up at me with desires she didn't even understand. She was innocence and danger all wrapped in one. She was alluring at best.

Isabella held a powerful spell over me, one that could easily take my heart on a frantic roller coaster ride. One could say I was falling for her, but if I were honest, I had already fallen for her. Alzerro was right, she was beyond worth letting go of my fears and worries.

As the days passed, I felt myself growing closer to her, as she seemed to be growing further away from me. Not in a sense that she was distant, but I could tell there was something festering in her mind. My cock was hungry for her at every passing glance, so much so I

INVINCIBLE

had fucked her three different times in the past twenty-four hours. However, now I sat awake in the chair across from the bed in her bedroom while she slept under the lights I had hung up for her.

She looked so small in the bed under a sea of white blankets. Her hair was a dismantled mess of blackness and her lips were parted ever so slightly as if she were fully worked over. *I bet she was having the best sleep of her life.*

I leaned back in the chair, the beer in my hand cool and heavy. I had forced myself through the ringer, never living a life that was all that satisfying. I was fake. Ever since I found out about Bree years ago. I lost touch with things, with people and with my feelings. Isabella brought back those feelings. She made me aware of what I was missing in my life.

I took a drink of my beer, my heart pounding in my chest.

The last woman I had ever truly loved left me.

My fists clenched as sweat formed on my brow.

Stop. Don't think about it.

I ran my fingers through my hair, my head in my hands. Don't think about the past. Don't allow it to take you under.

I watched as she walked away from me. I watched as she went to the car. That was the last day I ever saw her. Her smiling face turned toward me as she got into the car and drove down the driveway. I should've been with her that day.

"Stop..." I whispered helplessly to myself. I couldn't relive the past when I had so much to live for in the future. I lifted my eyes to Isabella. I had her. I had this life.

"Jared?" I could hear her voice as if it were real—as

if she were truly here with me. I knew she wasn't though—I knew that because she was dead.

"You're not real." I pushed the voice away, not wanting to hear what it had to say. I just wanted it out of my head.

"I want you to know that I loved you more than life itself. That when I passed over, my only thought was if you could make it without your mommy." I squeezed my eyes closed. No, no!

"Life has a way of changing things, people really. My death should've made you stronger, not weaker."

I placed my hands over my ears.

"I love you, Jared, but it's time to let go. Let the past be the past. Find love and happiness with someone else. I want you to love with all your heart and never let go. I want you to love as if you have no fears, nothing to live for but the heartbeat of the person next to you. Remember where you came from and tell your father I love him. He's done an excellent job of raising you."

"It's not real, it's not real," I repeated it in my mind, yet I could hear her voice over my own thoughts.

"Please..." I begged, wanting it to stop.

"I love you, Jared," she whispered into the air, the feeling of mist against my cheek surged through my body.

When I opened my eyes, my beer bottle had fallen to the floor, my head leaned against the wall behind me, my eyes focusing in on the ceiling above me. There was wetness against my cheek trailing down my face, so I lifted my hand and wiped it away.

Tears? How could I be crying—better yet, why?

"Remember me..." The wind howled outside the window. Memories of my mother invaded my mind, and without warning, I found myself going into the

INVINCIBLE

living room to pull out old photo albums from our time spent together.

Blowing the dust off them, I opened the first one. An old picture was on the front page, worn from the years. It was one of my mom, dad, and me. A smile had formed out of nowhere and my heart swelled, filling with so much love.

I flipped further through the album, my fingers moving of their own accord. From my first steps to my first lost tooth to a picture of my mother and I walking into the sunset. Through the pictures, I traveled back in time.

Tears fell from my eyes without hesitation.

Tears from a funeral I never cried at.

Tears for a mother who I had lost all too soon.

Tears for a man who spent years being someone he wasn't.

I continued to flip through the photos, watching every memory I had with her come to life right on the pages. It was when Isabella's hand rested on my shoulder that I realized just how caught up in the memories I truly was. I hadn't even heard her enter the room.

"I'm sorry for waking you," I said gruffly closing the photo album and wiping away any remaining tears that had stained my cheeks.

"Shhh…" Her voice caused my eyes to drift closed. She crawled up onto the couch next to me, her body molding to my own. Her warmth enclosed me, causing the darkness inside of me to brighten just a little bit.

I smiled knowing the reason I was changing had everything to do with her. Still, a new fear was finding a way to the surface. I could feel her pulling away from me and I wasn't sure why. Every time I asked if something was wrong, she had said no.

"I think..." I started to talk and then stopped. Was I ready to tell her I was starting to fall in love with her? Or that I was already in love with her? We hardly knew one another. At least we hardly knew the good in one another. We knew all the flaws and the damage that had been done, but we didn't know any of the good.

"What?" She blinked, staring up at me. She was beautiful, full lashes, plump lips and a face that didn't need makeup to enhance its features.

"I think I'm in love with you." The second I let the words out, I could see the wheel inside of her head moving. What was she thinking? Did she feel the same way? Only our breathing could be heard as she sat beside me, unmoving. I wondered if she was going to speak or if her heart was feeling the same anxiety mine was.

"Jared, you make me feel something I never have in my entire life. You make my heart beat faster than it ever has, and you make me feel normal. Whole. Not only that but loved. To me, you're the home I never had."

Tears formed in her eyes. We were two halves of a whole set out on a journey to find one another through the darkness of life. It didn't matter that our paths were littered with different things, obstacles, or struggles. All that mattered was we had found one another at the end of the tunnel.

"You're mine," I whispered to her as I pulled her body into my own. It had taken me a long time to realize this, but she was the one thing I never knew I wanted.

To me, she was everything I had ever needed.

CHAPTER TWENTY-TWO

Isabella

WE WAKE THE next morning to a loud buzzing noise. I could feel vibrations against my back, but I ignore them, snuggling deeper into Jared's chest. *God, I don't want to wake up yet. I could lay in his arms forever.*

"Fuck!" He groaned against my neck, his scent already doing crazy things to my body. I could feel my lady bits grow to life with the sound of his voice.

"We could..." I suggested smoothly, rolling away from his body just a little bit. He smiled pulling me back into his warmth while grabbing his phone. He had an incoming text for another job, the same man we had picked up yesterday but at a different location.

My insides churned, my body grew cold, and I pulled away without thinking. I wasn't sure I could keep up the quietness. The need to confide in Jared was growing stronger as I couldn't shake the feeling something bad was going to happen, and this man would be the cause of it all.

"Hey, you come back over here…" Jared wrapped his arms around me, pulling me back toward him. I squealed as his hands rubbed against all my ticklish spots.

"Stop!" I protested while laughter spilled from my mouth.

"Do you promise to stay in bed with me?" He smirked, an eyebrow raised and his hand ready to attack at any second. I nodded my head yes, allowing him to release me. It was then I made my move jumping from the bed and running from the bedroom. I could hear his footsteps behind me, my laughs filling the air.

All fear went out the window when I was with Jared.

"Oh, no, you don't…" he yelled right before he gripped me by the hips and threw me over his shoulder, my stomach landing hard against his shoulder bones.

"Let go of me!" I ordered.

"No. You lied. Now you must face the consequences." He could hardly say a word without his own laughter interrupting him. The moment he put me down, I made another run for it only to be picked up again and bent over his knee. He wasn't going to do what I thought he was, was he?

"You better not!" I growled, attempting to move off his lap.

"Oh, I will." He smirked just as his hand landed hard on my ass. Three spankings later, and I was ready to murder him. He was lucky he had released me and ran away to get breakfast ready because if he was still in the room, bodily harm would have occurred. I slipped into a pair of jeans Taylor and Bree had bought me, combed my hair, and headed out into the kitchen where

I could smell eggs cooking.

"How's that ass of yours feel?" Jared teased. I turned my head sideways to him.

"You want me to Hulk slam you through the floor?" I raised an eyebrow in questioning. He might be bigger, but I was sneakier.

"Try me…" He laughed as he placed a plate of food in front of me.

"I already have, and if I could, I would get my money back." I stuck my tongue out at him. We were acting like a bunch of kids, but I didn't care. Being able to do things as we were was a sign of freedom, something I had never been able to experience before.

"Oh, no, you didn't…" He growled at me from across the island, which only made my laughter grow more. Giving him a smile, I dove into my food as he sat down with his. We ate in peace, stealing glances here and there.

After breakfast, our charade of laughter continued, joking and flirting back and forth until we made it to the pickup spot. It was there when I clammed up, becoming quiet as a mouse. My belly filled with anxiety as the door opened, the man's scent filling my nostrils.

"Thank you for once again coming on such short notice." His voice caused shivers to go down my spine. I was on high alert, my palms sweating as I gripped the side of the seat.

"Not a problem, sir," Jared responded his eyes on me, taking in my reaction, I was certain. He moved the Tahoe from park to drive, heading out toward the interstate. When the car hit sixty, my heart started to pound in my ears. Every mile taking us further from where we live had my nails digging deeper into my palm. I know if I don't stop, blood will be drawn, but

INVINCIBLE

the anxiety has already taken root.

"Turn here, please," the man in the backseat ordered. I turned my eyes to Jared to see if he saw anything wrong with his request. He just sent me a smile following his orders as if it wasn't a big deal, yet I couldn't help but feel something was about to happen.

"Drive ten miles ahead and then pull over," he told Jared once again. This wasn't part of the route so why was Jared not reacting to it? A million and one thoughts took over my mind.

We traveled further down the road, no cars passed by on the other side, which just pushed me that much further over the edge. Just when I didn't think I could take anymore, I hear the man's voice again, this time speaking Russian.

"будь готов." *I'm ready? Ready for what?* My head pounded as Jared slowed down, pulling off to the side of the road where the man requested to be dropped off.

"Thank you," he said. I swear time slowed down as everything seemed to flash right before my eyes. Jared turned around to reply, the mystery man leaning forward, the metal from the gun shining. Then I watched as he nailed Jared upside the head, his mouth wide open, but no words came out. I didn't think—I just react as my body shook in fear.

"Noooo!!!" I cried out, trying to reach him before his head smashed into the steering wheel.

"You're finally mine." His voice, his smell, it all came back to me. *He is the man I was sold to.* Panic seized me as I turned in my seat, but it was too late and I'm too slow. He gripped me by my hair, causing the back of my head to collide with the headrest as he reached around my front.

"You tried to run. You tried to deny me something

that was rightfully mine." His hand went to my throat, fingers digging into my flesh as the air slowly stopped entering my lungs.

"Now I will deny you the right to breathe." He leaned forward and even with the seat separating us, he still managed to get close enough so his lips were against my ear, his nose rubbing against my throat. I flailed in my seat, oxygen deprivation taking over. I could feel the life leaving me as the light behind my eyes grew darker.

There was no light bright enough to make us invincible to survive the injustice he will bring. After all, there was no fighting the inevitable. *I'm indebted to him.*

CHAPTER TWENTY-THREE

Jared

"WAKE UP." MY mother's voice said. I felt as if I were floating, my body caught between the clouds and the ground. I want so badly to float upward with her, but something was holding me back. Something was forcing me to stay where I was.

"*Be strong, son.*" Her words soothed me as her fingers glided over my head. I could feel her warmth caressing my skin.

"What's happening to me?" I asked, but I could only hear my words in my mind. This must be a dream.

"*Be strong, son. Be strong,*" she whispered, and it felt like her voice was cradling me.

"Get the fuck up," someone growled. I could feel wetness against my skin as I swallowed, my mouth feeling as if it had been filled with cotton balls. Confusion took hold and the world seemed to be spinning around me as I tried to gain ground on what is happening.

"You thought you could take her, fuck her, and be her lover without me knowing?" Blinking my eyes open slowly, I realized I was no longer in the car. Instead, I was in what looked to be a basement of some sorts. The days past came back to me, and as I tried to digest what had happened, fear took over.

"Where is she?" my voice cracked. Blood filled my mouth, but I didn't care. Pulling my hands, I tried to move from the position they had me in. I needed to get to her, wherever she was.

"Wouldn't you like to know?" A man with a ski mask settled down on his heels in front of me. I turned my head away from him not giving one shit about what he had to say. None of that mattered. Isabella was all that mattered and I needed to get to her.

"Let me fucking go," I yelled fighting against the chains they had wrapped around my body. I could feel wetness dripping off my face and onto my shirt. My eyes caught the sight of blood dripping, and I wondered what had taken place.

"No can do. See, you took something very important to my boss... And now..." I could see the gun in his hands, the sliver of it glistening off the small overhead light above us.

"Now what? You're going to kill me? People will come for me," I taunted, narrowing my eyes. The chains were biting into my flesh as I pulled against them once again. I knew better than to let my guard down than to appear hopeless in this situation. *If you are taken, never allow them to break you or make you feel helpless.* Zerro's words echoed throughout my mind, things he once told me when I worked for him. Things I'm sure he tells his team now.

"No one is coming for you. Are you kidding me?" He laughed loudly and right in my face. "You're a nobody. In fact, once my boss comes in and tells you the news he wants to personally deliver, I'll be able to kill you." His voice was sick and twisted. Dark and distraught. There was no saving someone like him. Death would be his only saving grace.

I flexed against the restraints wanting them to fall to the ground in pieces. The creak of a door opening across the room startled me, forcing my attention to it.

"Sir." The man in front of me stood at attention as if he hadn't just been smarting off. I knew who to expect once the man stepped into the light. I also now knew the whole thing had been a setup. I should've been paying attention. I should've realized what was going on. Now I knew why Isabella was acting so strange.

"Welcome back. I thought the hit you took to the head might have taken you out altogether, but it is nice to see you coming around." He smiled, his white teeth glowing. His eyes were dangerous and evil, his body clothed in the same suit he had been wearing when I picked him up. Nothing seemed out of place on him.

"Give her to me!" I growled. They could kill me if they wanted too, but there was no fucking way I was letting them get out of here with her. Rage was about to take hold and I didn't know if I would make it out of here alive with her if I allowed it to take over.

"You seem to think I give a shit what you want." He removed his jacket, and the two men off to the side stepped forward, pulling on the chains that imprisoned me, forcing me to come to a stand.

"No, I know you don't give a shit. I'm just telling you if you think you have a shot at getting out of here with her, you're fucking wrong." My blood boiled as

INVINCIBLE

they pulled the chains tighter. With his sleeves rolled up, he swung at me. The momentum from the hit forced my cheek to turn, the knuckles of his fist scraping against my ear and cheekbone. Blood filled my mouth as I clenched my jaw.

"I own her, she is my property!" he yelled, gripping me by the throat.

"That's the funny thing about this…" I could see the frustration in his eyes mounting. He was ready to blow.

"Weird. I don't seem to find anything about this funny." His hand tightened making it harder to breathe. I smiled, knowing he couldn't kill me outright. He might have rage toward me, but there was no way he would kill me without Isabella here. He had a point to prove. He wanted her to know she had done wrong.

"I do…" I wheezed. "I think it's funny that you think…" blood pooled from my mouth again, spilling over and dribbling down my chin, "…you can own a woman in this day and age. I also think it's funny you think you have the upper hand here." I narrowed my eyes. "Kill me, I dare you." His smile was cruel as he pulled his fist back, delivering another hit to my head. Nausea filled my belly and my head started to spin as stars formed behind my eyes.

"Did you touch her?" he screamed at me. I smiled as my mouth filled with more blood. I spat it at his feet, aiming for his shoes and barely missing them.

"You mean take her virtue?" I had still managed to make a joke of this man. Nothing he was saying mattered to me. His questions were nothing to me.

"Knife," he ordered one of his men who handed one over promptly. I could hear the door creak open again, my eyes catching a glimpse of dark hair and I yelled.

"Isabella!" Her eyes flickered as she tried to escape the man who had his hand wrapped around her arm tightly.

"How dare you talk to her!" the man before me screamed, the knife in his hand coming down and entering my thigh. A burning sensation radiated through my leg as I howled out in pain, my leg going limp beneath me. Sweat formed on my brow as the burning continued.

"Stop, stop!" Her voice was broken, her eyes bleeding into my own. "Don't hurt him. Please. I will do whatever you want." She eyed me with tears in her eyes as my chest heaved in another breath. I felt the need for sleep taking over my body as each second ticked by.

"Don't give yourself over to these monsters." The words came out a gurgled mess. I could see the light overhead dangling, coming in and out, as I fought the haze threatening to take me under.

"Just can't get enough, can we?" I heard the man speak again, this time calmly right as another knife was plunged into my leg. Pain seared me, causing my body to convulse. I screamed out, feeling the pain taking me under.

"No! Jared! Hold on..." Isabella screamed just as the lights in my world went out.

I wanted to tell her how much I loved her and how she had taught me something so important in life...

But I never got the chance.

CHAPTER TWENTY-FOUR

Isabella

"JARED!" I SCREAMED his name praying he could hear me, praying he would lift his head and his eyes would be looking back at me.

Instead, they were closed and his body slouched toward the floor. They let the chains go, the clanking causing my nerves to raise more.

"How could you? I said I would listen if you let him go." The tears fell from my eyes without thought. Jared couldn't survive those kinds of wounds without medical attention.

"You have to save him." I fought against the man holding me back. The man I was promised to now known as Israel crossed the room, his footsteps heavy against the concrete flooring.

"I owe you nothing!" He gripped my chin, Jared's blood covering his hand causing my stomach to convulse. "He will die because of the things he has done. If you decide you don't want to listen, then I will punish you as well and believe me..." His other hand slid up my thigh. "I will enjoy it very much." I narrowed my eyes in anger. He was a snake, a dirty evil snake. I pulled my chin out of his hand, barely catching myself from falling to the ground.

Israel turned his attention back to a lifeless Jared. I could see his chest moving up and down but for how much longer? I could hear the thrumming of my heartbeat in my ears, the saliva in my mouth building up and the sweat on my hands forming.

"Get him up," Israel ordered and his men lifted Jared immediately, removing the chains and allowing his body to slump to the floor.

"You don't have to do this. It's not his fault this happened. He was just told to do something for a..." I tried to come up with a lie, but my mind went blank. I had nothing to lie about, nothing to say that could get us out of here.

"Do you think I'm dumb, little girl?" He crossed the distance between us, his hand ripping into my hair as he gripped it forcefully causing the skin to pull tight against my scalp. His dark eyes narrowed as he held my shaking body against his own.

"Do you?" he growled, his eyes lingering on my lips.

My stomach twisted in knots, agony taking over. It didn't matter what I did, what I said or didn't say— Jared wouldn't be walking out of here alive. Both our lives were over the second we got in that car.

I shook my head no, answering him before he decided to do something far worse to Jared. Tears spilled from my eyes and I shuttered as I watched his eyes follow the stream of tears down my face. There was no remorse or caring nature in them. Just pain, agony, and the need to feed on others.

"Tears? Tsk, tsk, tsk. They're weak!" he screamed in my face, his hand raising and landing on my cheek without warning. My skin burned from the strike as I fell to the floor, crumbling into a million tiny pieces. "You're weak!" he screamed into the air, his hands held above his head.

"Remove them both. Get them out of my fucking sight before I kill them." He pushed past one of his men, the force almost knocking him to the ground.

"Get up," the man next to me ordered. I turned my face toward him, allowing him to see the fresh bruise I could feel forming on my cheek. Is this what he stood for? Is this what he wanted for his life?

"Help us…" I begged, my voice a whisper as I prayed Israel wouldn't hear me. My eyes pleaded as his eyes bled into mine. I could see the apprehension in them—he wanted to help, but something was preventing him.

"Don't be dumb," he growled, his hand weaving into my hair as he pulled me from the ground by it. Rage formed in my veins—hate and anger formed from the pain they were causing me.

"You're a monster! A pathetic, disgusting, degrading, evil fucking monster!" I screamed as tears fell from my eyes. I could hear the room grow quiet and feel the tension pulling tight like a rubber band. They wanted to hurt me, they wanted to break me down. I couldn't let them.

"What did you say?" Israel twisted around, his eyes filled with anger and madness. A shiver ran down my spine. I should be afraid, I should be scared, maybe I even should've kept my mouth shut, but doing so would have given him more power over me than he deserved.

"I said…" I narrowed my eyes at him, "you're a pathetic," pulling from the man's hold on my hair, feeling it being pulled but was past the pain, "disgusting," leaning forward as I watched him step right in front of me, "degrading," I spat the word at him, no fear in my voice, "evil fucking person who gets off on hurting others."

My eyes glazed over as one last single tear fell from my eye. I saw the blur of his hand coming toward me but had no time to move—either that, or I felt no reason to do so. If he wanted to kill me, he would.

"You have made a grave mistake disobeying me." One hand wrapped around my throat while the other forced my eyes to meet his. Air is forced out of me as he squeezed tighter and tighter. My mind felt foggy as the light behind my eyes dimmed. I continued to hold on, gritting my teeth as my body started to sag from the loss of oxygen. My eyes flickered between a state of consciousness and unconsciousness. My body felt heavy, my mind unfocused, yet I clung to the chance to let him know he hadn't won.

"When you wake, your boyfriend will be dead, your body will belong to me, and your mind will be nothing but useless."

It was with his final words I could no longer hang on. I was gripping at the rocks along the side of the cliff, begging myself to stay, attempting to force air back into my body.

Don't let him win.

Those words echoed to me inside my head as I tried to move my hands, anything to keep me alert.

"Stop fighting it. Stop pretending you don't crave

me or the darkness I can and will offer you." I could feel his lips against my own, and it was then I let go.

Let go of the pain, the hate, and the anger that was holding me to the earth.

CHAPTER TWENTY-FIVE

Jared

MY BODY FELT as if it had been slammed through five floors of concrete, my legs numb from enduring hours of pain. The cold concrete beneath my face cooled my skin. I could smell my blood in the air and taste it on my tongue, but through it all, my mind was still drifting to Isabella.

You've failed. You've failed to protect her.

I clenched my fist against the concrete. I had no strength left. Just pain and a desire to make those who had hurt us pay. My head pounded loudly in my ears doing nothing to ease the ache. Air filtered into my lungs at a snail's pace as I heard footsteps off in the distance.

"Jared." The way he said my name had me pushing up onto my arms even if I knew they would give out against my body weight. I had to show him he hadn't won—I had to try.

INVINCIBLE

I grunted, unable to find my voice, my tongue sticking to the roof of my mouth.

"Interesting. Here I thought you died on us." I couldn't see him, even as I looked up. The light above forced me to blink my eyes closed the minute I opened them.

"I'm tougher than that..." I moaned. My legs burned and I could feel the blood flowing from the open knife wounds as I tried to move them.

"Tougher than I thought maybe..." he paused, "or just extremely fucking stupid." I never saw the kick coming until it landed on my stomach. Spasms of pain rocked through me as I tried to catch my breath.

"Do what..." I heaved in a breath, my chest aching, my stomach threatening to revolt all its contents onto the ground, "...you need to do to me, but let her go." I attempted to make a bargain with him.

"Pick him up," he ordered his men. They did as they were told, both men grabbing onto one arm each. They lifted me up, dragging me across the floor and pushing me down into a chair in the middle of the room.

"Look at me," Israel stated. I had no idea what his name was until I heard Isabella begging him to stop. I narrowed my eyes as much as I could, my head down toward the floor. He could beat me, destroy me, attempt to kill me, but he would never take the love I had for her away.

"I know things—things about you. Things not even you know... things about your mother." My head snapped up the moment I heard what he had said. I would be lying if I said I didn't want to know what it was he thought he knew, but in the same instance, I knew there was no way anything he was saying could be considered true. He was evil, a bastard of a man who got off on hurting people.

"I don't believe you," I growled, just barely getting out what I wanted to say. He smiled and it was sinister, dark, and ugly just like his soul.

"You can say all you want, but once I'm done telling you what happened, I doubt you will be able to not believe me." I ignored his words trying my hardest to push them from my mind all while he paced the floor in front of me. His fists clenched and there was anger in every single step. He hated how he had no control over me, and it only boosted me up more.

"Anything you say to me is a lie," I spat at him. "Nothing you could ever say to me would make me think what you're doing right now is okay. *Nothing.*" I made sure he heard me, my voice cracking as I raised it.

I watched as Israel grabbed a chair from the corner, moving it to the center of the room and taking a seat.

"Your mother was a sweet woman. Was she not?" He smiled.

He's baiting you. Don't give in.

"It's a shame how she died really…" His voice was dark.

Make it stop. Make the pain go away.

My head pounded in agony as my mind drifted between the past and present. Pain settled into my chest. Though my mother had died years ago, the pain of losing her could still be felt today as if it had happened yesterday. I didn't want to relive a moment of that with this man.

"Stop talking about her as if you knew her! You know nothing more than what you read on paper," I hissed out, lifting my chin. He held his hands in his lap as if he were unfazed by all of this.

INVINCIBLE

"There you go assuming things you have no idea about." He laughed, his voice filling the room.

"Assuming is not knowing, I knew everything about my mother. It is you who is wrong," I growled, pushing out of my chair. My legs wobbled, searing pain filling my body as I watched him.

"Jared. Dear fragile Jared." His hands were clasped together behind his back as he stood easily.

"Never talk of her as if you know her." I wanted to scream, but my voice failed to come out in any other tone but gravely. I was growing weaker by the second.

"When I found out who had my property, I did some digging on you. I needed to, needed to have something to shove down your throat when I got my hands on you!" He was screaming right in my ear, his saliva hitting against my skin.

"You have nothing because everything you're saying is false. You're a liar. Right down to your bones. You think you know her and you have a secret that was withheld from me!" I screamed with the last of my strength. I watched as Israel raised his hand, and with a sharp blow to the head, I fell to the ground, my body bouncing off the cement.

The clicking of his shoes on the ground sounded loud in my ears. The world before me was going in and out. How could I make it through this? How could I survive this? Would I even?

"The problem is this is a long running issue. You see, your mother was someone just like Isabella. In fact, you should be the property of my father..." A kick landed against my abdomen, but I felt nothing.

I couldn't feel any more pain at this point. He bent down with his fist pulled back. My eyes blinked in and out, unfocused as to where he was. I could feel his fingers digging into my skin though, and it just enraged me more. I was a caged animal inside my own body.

"Your mother's sweet cunt belonged to my family. Her parents sold her to us." He laughed and it was dark. Then his words hit me, and it was as if an ice bucket of water had been dumped on me.

"YOU'RE LYING!" I screamed. I failed to feel the tears falling from my eyes. I could no longer feel any emotion or pain. After enduring so much, you tend to shut off that part of your body and that's the point I was at now.

He shook his head. "Nope, I am not. Your mother ran just as Isabella did and it enraged my father. He searched for her for years, but she hid herself well. All it took was one slip up and we had her. He was just going to bring her back to where she belonged when he found her with the likes of your father. To find out she went and birthed another man's spawn made it even worse. My father spared you and your father all those years ago, but you fucked that up. Your mother's fate and yours are going to end in very similar ways." I could hear what he was saying but couldn't care less. The effect of what he had previously said still lingered in my mind.

"Love doesn't end all evil, Jared. Love doesn't take away the injustice. It just makes things worse. For love, you will die."

"What happened to her?" I stopped him, wanting an answer before he finished me off. I couldn't handle not knowing after so many years.

He smiled, happy I had finally given into his charade, "Well, we killed her, of course. She ran from us and so we caused the accident that took her life. We cut her brake line. We drove behind her, right on her bumper. Little tap here, a not so little tap there. We distracted her causing her to swerve. She couldn't regain control of the wheel, she couldn't stop either because... snip, snip. That's the short version. Lesson being, you cannot run from the mafia and expect to live."

My mind was spinning. Was there a reason to even hold on anymore? Everything that had happened was planned? I had all but prepared my own funeral.

"Any last words?" His voice sounded like a whisper as I tried to pull myself from my mind. Had I done this to us? Had allowing myself to open up to Isabella caused this? If she never met me would I even be here?

I said nothing, not even as his fist came down against my skin. I could feel wounds seeping open as he broke my flesh, blood being spilled and in that blood was my heart, my strength to move on.

I was losing this war and there wasn't a damn thing I could do about it.

CHAPTER TWENTY-SIX

Isabella

SWEAT FORMED ON my brow as I felt his hands touching me. My stomach threatened to empty onto the bed sheets, but I held it back knowing I would be beaten again if I did so.

"Izabella," he said my name in Russian, his words laced in lust. I tried not to move as he moved his fingers up and down my back. They were cold and made me feel sick.

I didn't respond to him, which earned me a hard slap against my skin. I tried not to cry out, to let the tears fall from my eyes, after all, allowing him to know he was hurting me did me no good. He didn't care.

"Your friend's life is now lying in your hands," he whispered, his teeth sinking into the skin on the back of my neck. I had thought over the tactics, the ways I could get out of here alive. Nothing seemed possible.

"What do you mean?" My lip wobbled. I had

INVINCIBLE

prayed like never before for Jared's life. Prayed he could make it through this if he held on just a little bit longer. Israel's nails bit into my skin as I bit my lip stifling the cry.

"I mean, he will die if you fail to do as I want you to." Another nip to the back of my neck, which caused me to arch away from him and his touch. I didn't want anything to do with him. His touch, his smell, everything about him sickened me.

"What do you want?" I sneered knowing whatever he was going to ask me was something I could never come back from. If I crossed this line with him, I would forever remember the pain it caused. If I didn't, I would lose Jared forever. His blood would be on my hands, his life is gone, all because of me. *Forever.*

"I..." he trailed one finger down my back, "...want..." another finger moved with it as he reached my ass crack. I could feel him probing at my entrance, my body growing tense, "...this. I want this sweet asshole. I know he's had your cunt, but I know you wouldn't give him this." He pushed against my puckered hole, pressing one finger inside of me. I screamed, a cry falling from my lips. Pain ripped through me as he pushed his way into me repeatedly, ripping away at my walls. One finger turned into two, two turned into three, burning me from the inside out with each motion.

Tears covered the pillow below my face as I failed to fight against him. I knew better. I knew if I did, he would kill Jared right now. Instead, I went inside my own mind, forcing the thoughts and pain away. I wasn't here with this sick man. I was with Jared. I loved *Jared.*

Jared laid a kiss against my skin as I looked up into a pair of eyes that held the world. He was caring, loving, my everything. I could feel his hands rub up and down my arms as he tried to soothe me.

"What's the matter?" he asked. I couldn't even force the words out. Seeing him even in this state had me choked up.

"Next time you think about him or even wonder what it would feel like for him to touch you, I want you to remember this." I clenched my fist as his sick words broke through my walls while he continued to violate me.

You're not a victim.

You're not a victim.

"Look at me, Isabella." Jared forced my eyes to meet his. The sky above us darkened, the clouds were full of pain and hate. I looked at him, and I could see straight through him, deep into his soul, into the parts that made him who he was. To the parts I loved.

"You're a slut, Isabella. A dirty little slut. My slut." That voice. I shook my head back and forth, pushing my way back into my mind.

A raindrop fell from the sky landing coldly against my skin. I shuddered knowing it was God who was crying for us, for the things we had lost and the things we had found, but mainly, for the things we couldn't have.

"Remember, even in the hardest moments of your life, I'm with you. I'm right here inside of you, a part of you and no one can take that from you." I stared up at him, my heart thumping of out my chest.

"Do you hear me?" His fingers dug into my shoulder. Tears slid down my face. I wasn't sure why he was hurting me so badly.

"Do you hear me?" Jared's face morphed into the monster who held us captive, his voice filled with

INVINCIBLE

venomous rage.

"DO YOU HEAR ME?" Warning bells went off in my head. "I don't even know why I bought you, why I paid what I did. You don't follow directions, you don't react to my touch, and you're so hung up on that boyfriend of yours in the other room." His temper was rising, I could no longer feel his touch against my skin, but it didn't change how I felt about him. Hate still filled my veins as I failed to move.

"You're a disgusting human. I would much rather die than give into your sick needs." I lashed out, not realizing what I had said. I felt like a different person as if something inside of me had changed. Every time he smiled, a small piece of me fractured inside, it turned black, and I wondered if after this I would ever be the same, if I could come back from such pain, or if I would always be as broken as I was right now.

"I'm glad you think so." He undid his pants, allowing them to fall to the ground, his tie and shirt came next. I kept my eyes on the floor while he undressed. I didn't want to see his body. I felt him crawl into bed on the other side of me. *What the fuck was he doing?* I would rather sleep on the cold hard ground.

"I won't sleep with you. I won't do anything you want me to do. You might as well kill me. If Jared dies, I'm good as dead, too." I seethed. I could feel him creeping toward me under the sheets, so I scooted to the edge of the bed. His hands snaked out, gripping me by the arm causing me to fall back against him. I couldn't escape as he held me against his naked chest. My body froze, my mind telling me the situation was about to get much worse.

"You will learn to live without him because, if you don't, your life will be hell. I would rather have you alive. If you're dead, you're out of my reach. If you're alive..." his breath was against my ear, "...I can hurt you. I can make you fear me."

His hand wrapped around my throat as he bit down into the flesh of my neck. His hold was tight, causing my vision to blur as his fingers embedded themselves into my skin. I could feel my skin bubbling, forming the impression of his teeth as blood flowed out of my broken skin. The hardness of him rubbed between my legs as he held my thigh slightly upwards. There was nothing gentle about his hands on my body, nothing sweet.

"Keep your leg there. Do not move it or you will regret it." His voice was harsh as he growled into my ear. Little black spots invaded my line of sight as the grip he had only tightened. It was as if he kept me right on the edge of passing out and being completely coherent.

His hand reached up, and I could hear him spit into it. My stomach convulsed as I reached up, clawing at his hand. His hold released slightly, enough to allow me to take one deep breath before he was squeezing again.

The same hand that had reached up went back down as he stroked his cock behind me. I wished the mattress beneath me would someone swallow me up whole, taking me away from this torture.

"You will obey me in every way. Or you will wish I would grant you mercy by death."

Those had been his last words to me before he positioned himself at the hole he chose to claim. My mouth was clamped closed as I bit into the tissue inside of my cheek. Blood filled my mouth, coating my gums and teeth. He gave no warning as he entered me roughly. A scream escaped my lips as blood leaked from my mouth, dripping down my chin.

His strokes were merciless, shredding every part of me. Agony ripped through me as I felt as if I were being torn from one hole to the other. Tears stained my cheeks as I continued to scream for my life, praying his men would feel something, anything... my misery at the very least and save me from this monster.

He held me against his chest as tight as he could, his pace finally slowing down. The ache running through me eased up as I felt him pull out of me. Hot streaks of cum hit me on the flesh underneath my butt as he rubbed it into me, marking me on the outside as he had on the inside. My body was soaked with sweat, tears streaked my face, and blood coated my insides.

Time seemed to stand still as I lay next to him. I could hardly breathe as I waited for him to fall asleep. Minutes passed as his breaths turned heavy. I felt hopeless even as I felt his arms go slack against me. He was finally asleep, his arm slipping from my body completely. I lay still forcing my breaths to even out afraid that he may be playing a trick on me. Sweat beaded on my skin. I could feel the soft sheets beneath my body and worried even the slightest movements would wake him.

I held my breath, the air leaving my lungs as I slowly slithered out of the bed, and my feet touched the floor with a deafening sound. I turned around just in time to see him roll over and see my virtue of that hole staining not only his flesh but the sheets as well. I stood still, my presence alone feeling as if it was a bomb going off in the room.

Once I heard his breathing turn normal and saw his body unmoving, I picked up his pants from the floor. Bending down caused a new feeling of physical suffering to surge through me as the tears continued to flow and silent sobs screamed in my head.

I moved slowly, afraid if I moved too fast, I would be able to feel where he just was as if he were still there. Searching through the pockets of his pants, I hoped to find anything. There had to be something in here. *FUCK!* Nothing! I just wanted to scream at the fact I had come up empty.

I grabbed the jacket next, turning my back and then checking if he was awake every other second. I felt as if my clock was ticking, each second becoming my last. Then my fingers landed on something hard in the inside pocket of his jacket. I pulled it out, wrapping my fingers around the hard metal.

I turned off the part of my brain that said I couldn't or I shouldn't. I pushed my morals to the back of my mind. There was no right versus wrong at this moment.

Without thinking, I got back into bed, but instead of laying flush against his body, I crawled up it, the handle of the knife gripped tightly in my palm, the blade exposed ready to do whatever I needed to do.

I hovered over his body, his snores filling the room just as I felt blood trickle down my thigh. With my free hand, I wiped my cheeks, erasing the tears he had caused. He didn't deserve them, all he deserved was death, and I would be the one to deliver him to Satan at the gates of Hell.

I dropped my hand to my thigh, tracing my fingertips in the blood before lifting my gaze back to him. My hand reached forward resting on his cheek, staining him as I was. I dropped my hand back down, grasping the handle of the knife. With both hands wrapped around it, I lifted the knife above my head, holding it over his sleeping form. His chest rose up and down as life continued to fill his lungs.

I took one deep breath and thought about the throbbing torment my body was feeling. I thought about Jared's body chained up on the other side of the door, and I put every ounce of fury raging inside of me into that one stab.

The blade pierced his skin as his eyes popped open. He reached upwards, blood filling his throat. I could hear the gurgling as I pulled the blade from his body. I could see his eyes begin to turn vacant as thoughts of him invading my body clouded my mind.

I sat there, crouched over him as I leaned in with the knife still in my hand. I rotated my wrist, slicing him across the throat.

Blood seeped out of the wound, purging my soul of his intrusion. The light in his eyes dulled before dimming out completely and glazing over. The rising of his chest slowed. I watched as he exhaled, waiting for his next draw of an inward breath, but it never came.

I took everything from him with one stab and slice of a knife. I watched him bleed out, and with it, so did the fear he once caused to stir inside of me.

CHAPTER TWENTY-SEVEN

Jared

A MUFFLED SCREAM traveled through the air bringing me back to the here and now. I could hear every noise, even the rats scurrying across the floor—the men snoring, the chains clinking together as I tried to move, but all I could think of was the scream I had heard. I knew it was hers, and that caused my stomach to clench tightly. *What was he doing to her to cause such a sound to escape her lips?* I jerked against the chains, trying to break free as I stifled my moans, just barely able to keep quiet. Pain radiated throughout my body. I was sweating, probably running a fever from my injuries. My clothes clung to my skin along with my own blood. The air around me stirred as coldness settled into my bones.

The realization there was no way I could get out of these chains without help forced me to sit in silence, my chest aching with every breath that escaped my lips as I looked up at the high window to the right. I begged for something, anything to happen so I could get out, so I could save Isabella and escape.

I scanned my surroundings, one of my eyes was swollen shut, and the other was barely open. I attempted to blink, a shadow cast across the window through the moonlight and into the warehouse. I knew something was going on, I could feel it in my bones. It couldn't be, could it?

I watched through unfocused eyes as two men pushed through the window. They did so with little effort and no noise. They were as quiet as the air I was breathing. As the window opened, two ropes fell from the opening. I forced myself not to move or scream out and tell them I was here down below, afraid the men next to me would wake up and see them before they could get inside. I couldn't risk blowing their cover, couldn't risk the lives of not only all of them, but mine and Isabella's as well.

How they found us is out of my mind, but if anyone could, it would have been them. I don't even know how they knew we were missing—let alone how they could pinpoint our exact location. My only guess was Zerro had a man on us or some sort of surveillance.

The men landed on the floor just as I heard the opening of the door to the room I knew held the one person who was keeping me alive. I was praying nothing had happened to her, but I knew better. I just hoped she was still alive.

Angling myself sideways, causing the chains to dig into my wrists, I saw her. It was for a brief second, but I saw her. The moonlight falling against her body as I wondered how she had escaped from Israel and where he was at this very moment. Those are the thoughts that ran through my mind until my eyes caught on blood. It covered her hands and the knife that she gripped tightly as the blade was shining in the moonlight.

Her eyes were vacant, far from the woman's eyes I once knew. I watched silently as she took a step forward and her hand shot out, stabbing the guard in front of her. I witnessed the need for her to survive the moment the knife entered his flesh and I knew Israel's fate.

A scream filled the silent room causing everything to come to life all at once.

"Get up," someone yelled as everyone came to a stand. I couldn't tell where the men who had come in had gone. My eyes were stuck on Isabella's as I saw tears trickle down her cheek, the knife dripping with blood and still clenched in her grasp.

In a blink of an eye, guns were pulled and drawn. Bullets began to fly, whisking through the air. A chill ran over my body the moment I witnessed one hit her in the chest. My heart grew cold as the first tear leaked from my eye. It was at that moment I died.

"If you're ever alone, look to the sky and know that I will always be there."

The words played back in my mind as gunfire continued to surround me. My body was numb, my eyes glued to her lifeless body against the floor. I could see blood pooling as people screamed and yelled around me. How helpless I truly was as I was not even able to be there for her last breath.

"Kill them all," someone yelled over the fire, but I didn't care. They could kill me now. The one thing keeping me alive, the one thing fueling me to keep breathing was now laying on the floor dead.

"Jared!" I could hear someone screaming my name, someone who sounded very much like Alzerro. I couldn't respond, I was falling, falling off the edge. The cliff was right there, right within my grasp. If only I could reach it... if only I could push myself off it, to feel the wind beneath my body.

"I love you," she whispered, her lips falling against my cheek. It was as if I were being kissed by an angel. Her body was covered in white, her eyes bright. She was so warm, so beautiful, so alive...

"Jared! If you're still in there, listen to me, okay?" I could hear Alzerro, but I couldn't feel him. My body felt cold, my mind felt gone, and I wasn't sure if he was real or not. He stared at me with worry in his eyes.

"You're going to make it through this. You're going to hold on because if you don't... if you don't... I don't know what I will fucking do without you, man." Pain showed in his features, his voice full of emotion. I tried harder to focus on him, his words, his hand against my flesh, but I slipped out of it again.

"Always know it was you who caused me to open up. It was you who took the hurt and pain away. You made everything worth living for." Tears were falling from her eyes. The warmth surrounding her was diminishing. What was happening?

"NOOO!!!" I cried out, my hands reaching for her. I could feel her slipping away, and I, too, wanted to go wherever it was she was going. I couldn't let her leave me. Not again.

"Stay with me," I begged. Her image was going in and out, her face full of sadness.

"You have to let go... You have to let ME go." She seemed hurt, angry, pained even. I shook my head no, holding onto her with everything inside of me.

"*It's not your time, Jared.*" My mother flashed before my eyes, Isabella's body drifting away from my own.

"Bring her back," I screamed, my body floating further away from her. A hand so soft I almost didn't feel it landed on my own.

"She will be fine, Jared. It is you I'm worried about. It's not your time yet. You haven't fulfilled your duties in life." I stared at her confused. What did she mean? The very reason for my breathing was lying on the floor, unmoving.

"JARED!" I could feel someone beating against my chest. I wanted to reach out to them. To entangle my hand with theirs and let them pull me back, but I refused. I felt content where I was. There was no pain and no agony.

"You're going back. You don't belong here." My mother whispered. I stared at her—my eyes had to be deceiving me. She looked just as she had the last time I saw her. Her dark hair long and wavy, she smiled and my whole world grew bright. I couldn't help myself. I had to wrap my arms around her, had to feel her, to see if she was truly real.

"We are losing him!!" someone screamed right next to my ear. *Losing him?* I didn't understand what they were saying. What it all meant?

"Jared, come on! Come the fuck on! Fight it, man. You got to fight it. Please, man, just come on." Alzerro was right next to me, trying to get me to come back to him. I wanted to ask him what it was that I needed to come back for but faded out again.

"The moment I knew I was dying, I thought of nothing but you." My mother ran her fingers through my hair and down my cheek. She smiled at me as if she were proud to see her son all grown up.

"I needed you. Why did you have to die?" Now I was the one crying, the one gripping her like a lifeline.

INVINCIBLE

She was fading, but I held on long enough to hear her next words.

"*You're exactly as I wanted you to be. You're strong, handsome, and I'm so very proud to have been your mother.*" Her lips fell against my forehead, and in that touch, I felt love as I had never felt before. I felt connected to the earth and the sky all at the same time. I was grounded but floating.

My life flashed before my eyes, brief moments throughout my life. I was riding my bike, smiling back at both my parents at six. The next flash was the first time I met Alzerro, and then I was opening birthday presents with my family the year before my mother died and witnessing my father full of love when we found out about Bree. And then, finally, it was the moment my heart started beating—when Isabella entered my house, and when I felt her body pressed against mine, or the first time I kissed her lips...

The air swirled around me as I felt pain like I had never felt before. It severed every nerve in my body, agony ripping my veins, as I had never felt before.

It was all coming back to me.

I was being brought back to life.

I was living.

I was breathing.

I was here.

CHAPTER TWENTY-EIGHT

Isabella

THE BEEPING OF machines, the smell of medicine, blood, and bleach filled the air. I hadn't moved from the hospital chair since I came into the room seventy-two hours ago. In fact, I hadn't done anything but stare at the man I loved in hopes he would awake.

We had been in the hospital for a week now. After the rescue, my life repeated the same things it had after my first rescue. They rushed me to emergency care as they checked me over, doctors running test and conducting evaluations on me within the first twenty-four hours. They tried to ask me what happened in the room before all hell broke loose. I didn't want to tell them. I didn't want anyone to know. To know he had taken something from me I would never get back, but I knew they knew. They just wanted me to tell them, to give the police my statement, but I couldn't. Just like I couldn't tell them I had stabbed him. That I had watched the life bleed right out of his disgusting eyes. I didn't want them to know that either. Worst of all, I didn't even feel sorry for doing it. I didn't care that I was killing someone. No remorse at all as I inserted the knife into him.

"Just because he isn't awake doesn't mean he's dead. He suffered a major head injury. His body needs time to heal. He'll wake up when he has rested enough," Alzerro said out loud, ripping me from my own tormenting thoughts. Jared's chest moved up and down, but he was unconscious to the world.

Upon his arrival, he had emergency surgery. They needed to reduce the swelling around his brain before putting him in what they called a medically induced coma. So I understood what Alzerro was saying and what the doctors had said, but it didn't change how I felt. It didn't change the pain that was radiating out of me.

The first three days of my stay here, I wasn't allowed to leave my room. I had suffered severe anal tearing and they wanted me bedridden. The whole time I kept asking for Jared, pleading with Alzerro to give me something. On the fourth day, he finally gave in and walked me down to Jared's room.

Flowers, balloons, and greeting cards decorated every available surface in his room as his family surrounded him. How they had all managed to get in this room without the nurses having a fit was beyond me. Whenever Bree, Tegan, or Zerro would visit me, they wouldn't let more than two of them in at a time.

"What is sitting here, being silent and unwilling to talk going to do?" he asked, once again pulling me from my thoughts as he questioned further. As if I would open up to him with how he was talking to me. I knew the only person I wanted to talk to was unable to do so. Until he was awake, I wouldn't say anything about what happened. He was my resolve, my reason to keep on. I couldn't blame myself for the things I had done.

"When he wakes up, I will talk about what happened." My answer was straight to the point, cold and callous. When would I be able to turn my emotions back on?

Never. You'll always blame yourself. If he dies, it's your fault.

"Why hold in the hate? The pain?" Alzerro tilted his head at me in wonder. Why was I holding onto the pain, the hate? Because holding on to it gave me something to hold *on to*. In a way, it grounded me.

"I can see the guilt in your eyes!" Alzerro's voice grew dark. "I can see it. I can see the blame written all over your face." He took a step toward me that forced me to go into my shell, to shut down.

"When you look at him, you see the mistakes you have made. You feel at fault when there was nothing that you could've done."

He's lying. It is your fault. If you never loved him, then he wouldn't be dying. If you didn't love him, maybe he would be here right now.

"Admit it!" he yelled as he clenched his fists beside him.

"There is nothing to admit," I said coldly, my eyes on the floor. I didn't want to explain my emotions. I didn't want to admit the pain I was actually feeling. If I talked about it, then it was real, and I didn't want it to be real.

Alzerro shook his head. "You're a liar, and if you would just open up, and let someone in. I just want to help you."

INVINCIBLE

Help? I wanted to laugh at the very sound of that word. Just over a week ago, I had been stronger than I ever had been. I had overcome so many obstacles, I had learned life was only worth living if there was meaning behind it. However, when you've been violated... when you've killed someone, when you've felt the life leave someone's body at your hands, it changes you. It makes you different.

"We know you killed him." The words slipped from his mouth like a secret that should've never been spoken. Those words caught my attention, causing me to look up at him through the strands of my hair as tears threatened to fall from my eyes.

Death.

I had caused death. I had killed, and I didn't even feel bad for doing it. If I looked in the mirror right now, I wouldn't recognize myself, yet everything Alzerro was saying was true.

"I did kill him. I don't regret it either." My face was void of any and all emotions.

"Then talk about it. Let it out." I looked into his eyes and knew he understood the emotions that plagued me. He understood how I was feeling, but still, something was holding me back from moving on. Something was holding me back from letting the gates open.

"I can't," I muttered, sinking back inside myself.

He will never get this part of you.

"There is more. Isn't there? That's why you can't open up? Fuck!" His anger filled the room, pushing the sadness to the back. He looked at me in a conflicted nature, and I wasn't sure why.

"When I...." He crossed the room pulling out the chair next to me so he could sit. His eyes darkened as he traveled back in time. "Ummm... it was normal for me in the world I was brought up in to witness men bring women back with them to their rooms. These women didn't care if they were passed around or shared. They wanted to have a good time. Most thought they could eventually become a wife and have the power of the mafia behind them no matter what because they needed protection, security." His voice seemed so off in the distance. "I never knew what went on behind their closed doors until I found one of the girls. She was sitting in a corner crying. she had been raped and beaten. It hadn't changed my ways, I was still pretty ruthless, but it had made me look at women differently. Even if I didn't want to admit it."

Sweat formed on the palms of my hands. I was bursting at the seams to tell someone, to let the pain out—but I couldn't. It felt wrong in so many ways.

"If he hurt you or if he touched you..." He struggled through his sentence. "If he did anything to you, please, please tell me. The doctors can't because of patient confidentiality, but you can." I could see the begging in his eyes, the pain he felt as he relived that moment. I blinked my eyes closed remembering the moment Jared had been shot. The misery, the agony that crossed his face. He looked as if he thought he was going to lose me.

Without muttering a single word, I nodded my head yes. Heavy tears filled my eyes and fell, landing against my skin with a hard thud. In those tears, I felt as if the weight of the world had been dropped off my shoulders.

Alzerro stared at me, fury burning in his eyes before wrapping his arms around me. He was hugging me, trying to glue me back together, and I let him. I let him squeeze me tightly as if he could push all the pieces into their spots, and though I wanted to be healed, I knew that if I lost Jared, it would never happen.

"I'm so sorry, so fucking sorry, Isabella." We sat like this for what seemed liked minutes as he continued to comfort me.

I glanced over at Jared, lying in the bed on the other side of the room. All the things I had done for us to be here right now, he had to wake up. He had to because, if he didn't, it would have all been for nothing.

"I think you should let the police know, and you should talk with a doctor about what you are feeling. You don't want to keep that poison in. It will destroy you if you do..." Alzerro insisted as he spoke to me softly. I didn't want to relive the moment that man shattered me over and over again or see the pity come across the doctor and policemen's faces, so I held my ground as I shook my head no.

By the time he let me go, I had already crawled inside my head again. I could tell by the somber expression marring his face that my admission had affected him in some way. I watched him as he walked over to Jared's bed, grabbing his hand in his own and squeezing it tight. After that, Alzerro sat with me a little bit longer before saying his goodbyes.

Nurses and doctors came in and out throughout the night, checking on both Jared and me even though I said I didn't need anything. As time passed by, I found myself moving closer to Jared. I sat in my chair right next to his bed and closest to the window, watching the room grow dark. A calmness settled over me when the night sky appeared. It was as if I craved the darkness, as if I dwelled and lived in it.

The pain would follow me for the rest of my life,

but nothing, and I do mean nothing, would kill me as much as losing Jared would. Those were the thoughts I replayed in my mind as tears rolled down my cheeks, and I held Jared's hand in mine.

The moment I felt him squeeze my hand, I knew I wouldn't dwell in darkness forever. I knew this pain was a temporary pain. And one day I would be whole again.

I would be me... *again*.

CHAPTER TWENTY-NINE

Jared

THEY SAY YOU should always measure life based on the moments that take your breath away, and in my case, it was the most accurate thing I had ever heard. *I had died.* I had seen and felt heaven. Felt my mother's kiss against my cheek and the love of my life being pulled away from me.

Nothing was as real as feeling—as physically feeling, someone else's skin against yours. As realizing that you had so much more to live for. I felt her hand in mine, I felt the love and sadness seeping from her and pouring into me, begging me to just wake up.

"I'm breaking..." I heard her words and felt her heart ache. I could feel my arms tingling, my hands on fire as her hand warmed mine. *I had to let her know I was here. That I was still inside.* I forced energy into my body as I squeezed her hand. Her gasp filled the room, and I knew she had finally felt it. She had finally realized I was still here with her.

"You're alive? You're in there!" She cried, and I could practically feel the tears rolling down her cheeks. I smiled internally as I lay trapped inside, unable to feel any other part of my body. I wanted to wrap my arms around her and cradle her body against my own. Instead, I listened to her cries and pictured myself comforting her in my mind, hoping she could feel it from here.

I felt her body brush against mine as she reached over me. The movement caused my eyes to pop open. I tried to swallow, but something was in my throat as I felt my heart start to throb inside of my chest. I stared at her, tears painting her beautiful face as the machines blaring around us.

A minute later, a nurse entered my room, probing and checking me over while Isabella told her how she squeezed my hand, and I squeezed back. How not even a minute later my eyes were on her. "Don't remove the tube on your own. I'm going to get your doctor!" The nurse's voice lingered in the air as she disappeared out the door. The moment we were alone again, Isabella's voice filled the room.

"I thought I had lost-t-t... I thought I had lost you. Thank you for coming back to me. I don't know what I would have done without you." Her lips pressed against my cheek. Her smell surrounded me, her body enveloping me in a mist of happiness. I had never felt so much emotion or passion in one kiss. I desperately wanted to speak, to allow everything I was feeling to flow from my mind.

When I thought she had been shot, I remember the feelings that coursed through me. I felt as if I had died myself, as if I were losing who I was as I watched her fall to the ground. But it wasn't she who had been shot. *It was me.* It was I who was falling to the ground, who had been shot, who was dying.

My mother's words cradled me as I fell from heaven.

"Remember who you are, Jared. Remember that the good always outshines the bad in people. No amount of darkness can smother the light." Her tears were so real, her warm arms wrapping around me.

She was real, everything about her was.

"I watched you fall to the ground. I thought everything I had done might not have mattered..." Her voice halted as she tried to choke back her emotions.

"My heart stopped beating. My mind started to think of ways I could have misunderstood what I had seen. I thought I knew what it was like to feel broken, but when I thought you were— God, I can't even say it! I knew then what it really felt like to be broken." The beeping of the machines filled the silence she had allowed to form between us before she continued on.

"I thought you were gone. You were. *You died.* I saw it with my own two eyes. You were shot in the chest. You were bleeding to death—there was so much blood. Blood everywhere. On my hands, on you..." In her voice, I knew something was off—that everything wasn't right. That something had happened and she didn't want to burden me with whatever she was carrying.

"It was a miracle really. I didn't understand how they had found us. I didn't know they were there... Alzerro said he tracked us by your phone and car. That-t-t he had put some sort of device on your GPS system in case something happened. He said, after calling you and getting no answer, he started to worry. That

INVINCIBLE

something told him you and I were in danger."

I smiled inside as my eyes stayed trained on her. God, we were so fucking lucky. I couldn't even picture what life would be like if we were still there.

Isabella's words played back in my mind.

You died.

I would still be dead.

Emotions continued to swarm me. I was breathing now, I was alive, and I had never felt more life flowing through me—more now than ever.

CHAPTER THIRTY

Isabella

TWO MONTHS HAD passed, and I still felt as if a part of me had been left behind in that warehouse. I had told Jared everything I could in between the tears that had escaped. He understood, so much so he hadn't touched me with more than a hug or a kiss. He didn't want to hurt me or make me feel trapped. He wouldn't even sleep next to me in fear I would have a nightmare thinking I was back in the warehouse.

That fear, that anger in his eyes as I told him what Israel had done to me and what I had done in return to him, I'll never forget it. Just like I would never regret taking Israel's life. They didn't charge me. In their eyes, it was self-defense, and the fact they had orders to kill him when they got their hands on him anyway. It didn't matter to them who took his life as long as he was no longer breathing. I had just done them and the rest of the world a favor it would seem.

INVINCIBLE

"Isabella?" Jared called my name so softly I almost missed it. I spent a lot of time inside of my head now. Words didn't need to be said between us as all it took was one look for him to understand where I was in my mind.

"Jared?" I said his name as I turned my head away from the television and smiled at him. I hated the distance he had put between us. Because of others, he felt even the littlest of things would push me over the edge.

He didn't realize he was the one thing that could cure the ache inside of me.

The memories.

"I love you." He pulled me from my spot on the couch and into his lap, his arms wrapping around me. The smell of soap and the intoxicating scent only Jared could hold filled my nostrils causing my body to come to life. Jared's nose nuzzled against my neck as he breathed against my flesh. He was calming me. He had done this numerous times as a way to relieve the stress. We both knew the good that being close could do for one another. To feel his breath upon me put my soul at ease.

"How are you feeling?" I barely got the question out. My body and mind were thinking about two very different things.

"I'm feeling…" a kiss replaced the warm breath against my neck, "…like I need to be close to you." Another kiss. "One with you." Another kiss. My mind was swirling, my body becoming a puddle of lust.

"It's okay now. I'm okay now…" I reassured him as he picked me up and turned me around to face him as if I weighed nothing at all. We now faced each other, our eyes bleeding into one another's.

J. L. BECK

"The moment I let you get underneath my skin was the moment I knew things would be different for the rest of my life." I could feel tears prick at my eyes. I wrapped my arms around him tightly, never wanting to let go.

"Shhh. I want my body to say the words I know I will never be able to. I want you to know how much I love you, not only with my touch but with my heart." He pushed the sides of my tank top down and blazed a trail of kisses across my chest. My body grew warmer with every kiss against my skin.

"Ahhh..." I moaned out as pleasure took over. Without blinking, I found myself removing my shirt, the frenzy to finally have our bodies meet one another's after two months of nothing. I healed, I was moving past it, but now I wanted to bare myself to him. I wanted to feel something other than the past. I wanted to feel his love in every single way.

Jared's hands roamed over my body as if he were painting our future and undoing the past. He gripped my waist, lifting me off him so he could unbutton his pants as I let my flowy skirt and panties hit the floor. I stood before him, naked and ready to take on the world.

"You're beautiful," he whispered. I watched his muscles flex and took in the scar on his chest that signified the pain we had endured—and what we were.

We were a miracle. He was a miracle, and our love was a miracle.

He stood up, pulled my body into his as he pressed his mouth against mine. His lips were soft, yet his tongue was harsh against my own as if we were dancing to the beat of our own drums. His hardness flushed with my softness, turned the simmering fire to a burning blaze. I wanted our bodies touching in the most intimate ways. I wanted to feel every part of him all over me.

"Are you sure? We can stop right here, we don't have to go any further if you don't want to. I can wait until you are ready," Jared whispered into my mouth, a moan slipped past my lips from him breaking our kiss.

"I'm sure. I want to give myself to you. I want our bodies to connect and become one again. Please, Jared. Give this to me." I whispered right back to him, reassuring him this was indeed what I wanted. What I crave, desire, and need as I wrapped my hand around his hardness. A roar escaped his lips, like a lion sending out a warning. It was rough and hard, vibrating through my body and going straight to my core as I squeezed him.

I stroked him once, twice, three times before his head snapped back and his eyes closed. I watched him get lost in the feeling of my hand enclosing him as I moved up and down his length. It was like the gun range all over again, a sexual aphrodisiac making me feel powerful.

The palms of his hands heated my skin while they ran down the sides of my body to the back of my thighs, causing a shiver to run through me as he lifted me off the floor. My arms wrapped around his neck, my legs around his waist. We stared into each other's eyes as he turned us around. Our bodies went down, and I hit the cushions of the chair softly, his body covering mine.

"You are what my heart longs for every single second of every day," he whispered the words to me as he entered me completely at a leisurely pace. I could feel every inch of him as he moved slowly inside of me, the pain mixed with pleasure, answering my carnal desires.

Forehead to forehead, our moans filled each other's mouth. His body was slick against mine, sweat beading over our flesh. His strokes gentle, yet powerful as he owned not only my body but also my soul. All of it and every single touch of his skin rubbing against my flesh made this moment so very passionate.

My thighs squeezed him closer, my core clenching tighter as he encircled my body with his. Driving in deep, pulling out easy. Over and over again. My nails dug into his back, his teeth nibbling on my shoulder as he rotated his hips. This was us… us giving ourselves to each other, I thought to myself as my body tingled from the inside out. It started as a tiny flicker of a flame in the pit of my stomach, flowing outward as a flush covered my body.

His breaths came louder, his hand gripping tighter as every one of my senses became overwhelmed by him. He didn't stop, not when I let go. Not when my body became wild and not when I felt as if I were flying free.

I was sensually wanton, moaning loudly, and begging for more as he whispered *"You're my light, angel"* and even then, he never stopped moving inside of me. He just kept going, reigniting my body all over again.

He made love to me, with not only his body, but with his words. Pushing me to the limits, making me feel like I had never felt before. Gentle and rough at the same time he brought me back to who I was.

He made me realize what it was I had found in him.

He made me feel what it was like to love someone and to be loved in returned.

I didn't ever have to fight the darkness alone again,

INVINCIBLE

and the days when I felt it would take me under, he was there shining his light on me just as I did for him.

We were flawed but real, and our love, intense and raw.

We overcame it all.

We survived the injustice.

CHAPTER THIRTY-ONE

Isabella

I PACED THE living room floor, my feet wearing a path through the carpet. I was so nervous Alzerro would say no, so nervous I would have to stay in confinement for the rest of my life.

"Rest easy, angel. It's all going to be okay, I promise." Jared comforted me with soothing words even if he knew there was a chance it wouldn't sway our way. It had been a few months since I had escaped hell and then almost lost Jared. I went to therapy every day and was on track, feeling better about myself and learning to let go of the past. Part of that letting go was getting closure from my parents. I had never been given that chance, and now... well, now, I wanted to take it.

Jared's ringtone blared loudly, and I stopped dead in my tracks, my eyes honing in on his phone as he answered it and smiled at me. He was sitting on the couch—all cool, calm, and collected, while I... I was

INVINCIBLE

what Bree would call a hot mess.

"Okay. Yes. I know." Jared rambled on, the time he stayed on the phone seemed to drag on with each word. My heart was beating out of my chest, my palms sweaty. I felt like I was breaking out of prison or something.

"Yeah, I'll tell her." My breathing slowed as Jared hung up the phone.

"Out with it," I ordered. His face held no emotion so I couldn't go off that. He continued to stare into my eyes, void of any and all emotion before a cheesy smile spread across his face. I knew then I was truly free.

"He said the Witness Protection Program has released you. There is no longer a risk to your life." He shot up from the couch, wrapping his arms around me. As happy as I was, I realized just what this all meant.

"Did he…" I paused, I was so afraid to ask, having been told no numerous times.

"He said it's your choice if you want to call them. You can't let them know where you are though, and you are only allowed to call them once…" He gripped my cheeks tightly, forcing me to stare directly at him. "I think it's the closure you need to move on." His eyes twinkled in the lighting. This had been the plan after all, to move on from the past. I needed to learn to let go of the pain, to forgive even if they weren't sorry. Allowing hate to rent space in my mind was giving people the power to destroy me without them even knowing. I couldn't allow that to happen anymore.

Jared pulled away from me, placing his cell phone in my hand. I cast my eyes down toward it as it weighed heavily in my hand. Could I do it? Endure the pain, open the wounds of the past, and push forward?

"You're only as big as your biggest fear," Jared

whispered as a reminder to me. I headed toward the patio door, giving him a short smile as I shut the door behind me. I slumped down into one of the chairs and punched in the digits to dial out of the country and block Jared's number. Once I had entered those correctly, I dialed the number I knew by heart. I wasn't sure if they would answer or not, but I hoped they would.

I pressed the send key and waited for the ringing to sound on the other end. There was a long pause of just air filtering through the line, which caused my heart to pound harder. Then the ringing sounded and I started to calm a bit. The phone was slippery in my hands as I pressed it to my ear, the ringing continuing.

"здравствуйте." A meek voice answered on the other end. I was so choked up, so unsure of what to say that at first I said nothing.

"здравствуйте?" Someone snatched the phone from someone else, the voice on the other end sounding much older, much more known and held an authoritative tone.

"Momma!" I cried out, unable to stop the emotions from coming forward.

"Izabella?" Her Russian was thick just like I remembered. She seemed stunned, even displeased.

"Yes, Momma! It's me." I spoke to her in English as tears fell from my eyes. I didn't even know—had no idea why I was crying. It's not as if they cared about me when I was there. Maybe it was the idea that I needed a small piece of home with me.

"How..." she questioned, her voice growing very quiet as she too spoke in English, "you're not supposed to call, child. Your duties have been done." Her admission caused my heart to split in two.

INVINCIBLE

"Is that…" I stumbled over my words, taking a deep breath. I didn't want her to know just how much her words hurt me. "Is it true? I mean—was this all you ever had planned for me? I'm calling after all this time to let you know I'm okay, and you tell me my duties have been done?" I was hurting, my heart wide open just like the day she let them take me.

Her breaths filled my ear. "Isabella, your sacrifice for your family was all we ever needed." Her words were final. It was as if she didn't even care. How had I thought for some reason she would? That she would say she was sorry, that she loved me and didn't mean for it to happen? All those things had been false hopes. She wasn't overjoyed to hear my voice, to know that I was still alive.

"How…" What did I want to say? Wasn't this about closure and allowing those wounds to scab over?

"How is Marcy?" I asked. I could hear her sighing over the phone as the line grew quiet for a brief moment before her reply came through.

"She is so quiet. Don't talk to any of us much and when she does, it is a simple yes or no. She is just as much a burden as you were." Her confession caused my blood to boil and I found myself snapping.

"Let me talk to her!" My voice was strong, not one trace of weakness in it. Marcy was the youngest of my siblings, yet at the age of six, she had more morals than most. We always had a special bond, since the moment I held her in my arms. I felt as if we were one in the same.

My mother sighed heavily into the phone once again, before yelling for her.

"Здравствуйте." The quietest voice I had ever heard met my ears.

"Marsi?!!" I questioned in Russian, almost

screaming her name as I allowed the happiness of hearing her voice hit me.

"Да?"

"I have missed you so much," I cried out, switching between languages. In my old house, this was nothing new as our father spoke to us in English. Even though he could speak Russian fluently, he only spoke to our mother in her native language.

"Isabella?" she screeched, asking in English as well. Had it been that long? Had time passed that much that she had forgotten what I sounded like?

"Yes, Marcy. It's me. It's Sissy!" I could hear her voice filling with emotion as she huffed a sob into the phone.

"I...I missed you..." I could all but see the tears falling from her eyes. "Momma doesn't do my hair like you did or take me for walks. She doesn't care, Isabella." Anger racked my bones. How had a six-year-old been able to gather all of this?

"I know, sweetie. I know... and I wish..." What did I wish? "I wish you were here with me. I miss you so much. You know that, right?" I prayed she knew it.

"I do... " Seconds passed before she spoke again. "I want to go wherever you are. I want to be with you, Izzy. I hate it here." More emotions swarmed her as she sobbed uncontrollably into the phone.

Through Marcy's heavy breathing, I could hear my mother screaming, her Russian sharp, which told me she was pissed off about something, which wasn't really all that much of a surprise.

"Momma is mad, I have to go..." She cried harder into the phone.

"подождите, Marsi... I won't leave you there. I will do whatever I can to bring you where I am. Okay?

INVINCIBLE

Don't give up. Just stay strong. Let me talk back to Momma. I love you." Her sobs seemed to stop as she realized what I had said.

"I know you'll come for me. I love you too, Izzy," She whispered into the phone just as my mother's voice came through the line again.

"What is it, Isabella? Your Poppa will be home soon. I need to finish dinner. You cannot call here again." Her words were filled with irritation as if I had just ruined her day.

"Вы не хотите Marsi, она такая нагрузка для вас, то вы не будете возражать мне получить помощь, чтобы получить ее здесь, со мной. Вы услышите от кого-то достаточно скоро, и когда вы делаете, делать все, что они просят вас. Marsi, будет моя ответственность в настоящее время." I whispered harshly into the phone right before the line went dead. I was shaking, my own fears and hate coming forward. I felt as if I was being swept out into the ocean. Ahead was a life jacket, but every time I reached for it, it seemed to float further from me.

Minutes ticked by as I sat in the chair, feeling the warmth of the sun against my body. I had an amazing life now, a man who worshiped me, and I was free to do as I pleased. I couldn't allow these feelings coursing through me to ruin all of the progress I had made.

"Are you okay?" I didn't even hear the door open behind me as Jared's voice lingered in my ears.

"If I told you I wanted to save my sister, would you tell me I was crazy?" I asked without hesitation.

"I would say that if that's something you want to do, if it's important to you, and it will make the healing easier, then I think you should do whatever you can." He took a seat next to me, and for some reason, I found myself crawling into his lap. I felt comfort in his arms as I had never felt before, the warmth always covering me like a blanket. It reminded me of where I was. *Here.* Not there.

"Then let's try. Let's talk to Alzerro and see if we can," I cried into Jared's shirt. The tears weren't sad ones, just ones that needed to be released. Ones that I had kept deep inside for so long.

"Whatever you want, Isabella." He pressed his lips to my forehead and I melted. *He was more than I had ever expected,* I thought as my last words to mother replayed in my mind, but this time in English.

You don't want Marci. If she is such a burden to you, then you won't mind me getting help to get her here with me. You will hear from someone else soon enough, and when you do, do whatever they ask of you. Marci will be my responsibility now.

* * * * *

1 YEAR LATER

"OUR ANNIVERSARY ISN'T until Monday," I said loudly, Jared's robust voice was rattling through the speakers of our car. I was on my way home from working at the women's center that I ran with the help of Bree and Tegan. We were offering our support in every way we could. Moral support, therapists, food, clothes, even housing for women who had been raped, kidnapped, or beaten.

I never knew so many women went through what I had been through. To help them healed me in more ways than one. When I learned the stories of Bree and Tegan, I cried. I cried for them, and for me, and for all the things we had all lost. When they came up with this idea, I was apprehensive, not sure I could help someone when I was still taking it day by day. At first, it was hard seeing these broken women every day, but as each day went by, I felt lighter. It got easier. We were all survivors and it fueled me to give them my all in their healing processes.

Bree had recently just come back to work after giving birth to their second child and then taking months off to spend time with both kids. Tegan was a little firecracker, swearing up and down that she wouldn't let another child rip her vagina apart, but Devon had other plans. You couldn't see it in his eyes when he looked at his daughter—like he was longing for another child.

The first time I met Devon was at the party Bree and Tegan had thrown for me. It was my *'Get out of Witness Protection Party.'* He pulled me to the side as everyone chatted and the girls played around us. As soon as we were off to the side where the noise wasn't overbearing, he pulled me into an embrace.

He told me it was wonderful to meet the woman who gave Jared what he had been missing. I just smiled at him, unsure of what to say as he stared into my eyes. Then he shook his head, as if he remembered a time that he wasn't very fond of before telling me he was so sorry he was just now officially meeting me, and he hadn't wanted to overwhelm me since seemingly we were strangers, so he had chosen to wait. Plus, with everything that had happened, everyone thought it was best to wait to introduce us until I was better so I wouldn't be uncomfortable.

He hugged me again and batted those forest green eyes at me, telling me not to bust Jared's balls too much.

I could tell he was the softest of the three men, but at the same time, you wouldn't want to cross him either.

Jared was now an exclusive driver, solely for Alzerro and Devon's teams. He was so much happier now, and that made me happy. He still had his days when he would try to shut everyone out, but then he would look at me and it was like his world altered. Our demons would probably always haunt us, but at least we would never be alone in the darkness to fight them ourselves ever again.

We weren't married and didn't have any plans for babies just yet, but who knew what the future held. Right now, we were just in love and together, helping one another put the pieces of our lives back together. We made a promise to each other, and for me that was enough. To me, our promise was just as valid and strong as the bond that a husband shares with his wife. That bond tethers us together in our own special way. Once we both are over the past completely, we will establish our future through marriage... But right now, we are happy where we are, plus we are still very much getting to know each other.

"Who cares? Every day with you is a celebration, baby. Plus you weren't complaining the other night when I had you all over my cock," he growled. My cheeks grew red, thinking about the things he had done to me. Being with him had awakened something in me. I had a deeper reason and need to fight—together we made each other whole again.

"Shut up, Jared." I smiled, and it was a huge one. He had me so caught up my heart was beating out of my chest.

"Where are you by the way?" he asked. I rolled my eyes, he had been asking that a lot lately, working overtime with Alzerro twice a week. He hadn't really been distant, but more closed off when it came to his work. I couldn't blame him though, the things he had to deal with as a driver for the FBI made even the thickest skin of people change.

"Turning onto the interstate," I lied. I was right down the road, but I wasn't going to tell him that. I wanted to surprise him.

"Okay, well, I'll see that sexy ass when you get home. Love you," he said. I said it back to him and then hung up. His words never got old. His *'I love yous'* never changed. In them, I could feel his love.

I pulled into the driveway, slipping from the car as quietly as possible. A smile lingered on my face as I headed up the driveway and to the door. Finding the key and placing it in the lock, I turned it realizing instantly that the front door wasn't locked at all.

Weird.

I pushed the door open and my entire world stopped. My purse and work bag fell to the floor as my eyes landed on my sister's small form standing in front of Jared. Her skin was a light shade of brown, her eyes and hair both dark just as mine was. Tears slipped from my eyes as I ran across the room, wrapping her in the tightest hug known to mankind. She squealed in laughter, squeezing me back just as hard.

"Is this real?" I said out loud. Jared nodded his head yes, which caused more tears to fall.

"We were able to work out the details a month ago after we got the paperwork straight. Since your dad is American, you both can be here because of citizenship laws and regulations. Your mother was just taking her sweet time signing over her parental rights to you, but she finally did. It took some time to transport her as well, but here she is." I wanted to hug him and kiss him, and... there just weren't words for what I wanted to do.

"I'm here to stay, Sissy..." She smiled up at me, and I realized, even if I hadn't been healed before, I was now. Having her here with me gave me more of a reason to try. Even if everything wasn't perfect before, it was now, at this exact moment.

We found peace in the things we couldn't have justice in.

# # #

READ ON FOR AN EXCLUSIVE LOOK AT

Worth The Chase

A BITTERSWEET AND KINGPIN LOVE AFFAIR CROSSOVER SERIES...

CHAPTER ONE

THE PAST

I REMEMBER THE very first time I ever saw him. My eyes lingered over his body, across his shoulders, and finally up to his face. His body was lick worthy. His abs were on full display for the entire Auburn University female population and, believe me, they were all looking.

His eyes were blue like the sky before a storm. Dark and full of pent-up energy ready to be unleashed on anyone who got in his way. His chin had slight stubble on it, his nose straight, and his teeth white. He looked like a GQ model. It was no wonder everyone, including myself, lusted after him.

"Gia. Focus on this shit in front of you. I'm here to tutor you, not have you check out my brother." Chance, Chases twin brother, scolded me. My cheeks warmed in embarrassment as I brought my eyes back down to my notebook and away from Chase and the blonde that was stuck to him like glue. The sun was shining through the trees and down onto us as the summer temps continued to rise. We were laying out on the front lawn of the campus working on Advanced Biology.

I needed to be focusing on cell splitting and not removing my panties and allowing that asshole access...

"Gia?" Chance said my name again, pulling me from my thoughts. At least I wasn't being yelled at for staring at his brother.

"What?" I answered lifting my face to meet his. Chance was gorgeous, too. He had the same body of his brother, except his eyes were green, and he had a softness to him, and he wasn't an asshole to everyone that even took a glance at him.

"You need to focus. Stop thinking. It doesn't matter if you're not looking at him. I can tell you're thinking about him which is the same fucking thing." His voice was full of frustration. I didn't know what to say. It was impossible to focus with him around. It was like Elementary school all over again, except I was a senior in college and needed to get my shit together so I could graduate with a degree that mattered. I had fought for my chance to go to college, I had begged and pleaded for a chance at this life, and I needed to stay on track. Even if being off track sounded so much more fun. Shocked that Chance had come at me about it so meanly, I closed my Bio book and grabbed my notebook.

"Focusing would be easier if you didn't bring him everywhere with you," I growled, narrowing my eyes. It wasn't Chances fault he had to bring Chase all over the place like he was a toddler. Chase just had a habit of causing problems.

"Oh, and you're finally done with the princess." It was then that Chase decided to butt in, the blonde missing from his arm as I picked myself up off the grass. I raised an eyebrow at Chance, showing him that this was exactly what I meant when I said it was hard to focus.

"You know my name is Gia. Use it or don't talk to me at all." I sneered. He was gorgeous and a delectable specimen, but the second he opened his mouth, I wanted to stab him in the eye with a fork. I wanted him for one thing and one thing only. I wanted to know if he was as good in bed as the rest of the girls on campus said he was. Aside from that, I didn't want to listen to him speak once.

He tilted his head sideways at me. "Wow. I just heard Chance having to remind you not to stare. Seems someone was a bit distracted." He mocked smiling, which kind of made me go weak in the knees but also made me want to throat punch him at the same God damn time. Of course, he would change the subject. He was good at dismissing the things he didn't want to hear, or have anything to do with.

If he thought I was going to play into his hand, he was wrong. I turned on my heel away from him, fully intent on heading back to my dorm. I had to be moved out in a month for fall classes, which meant I would be on the hunt for a new apartment with my best friend Taylor, who would be a freshmen this year.

"Wait... We need to meet up and go over the lab tests you'll be tested on this year one last time." Chance stopped me from walking away, which caused me to turn back around and face Chase, who had a shit-eating grin on his face.

Hate him for all that it's worth, I told myself. Don't look at him like a piece of cake you want to devour. No, look at him like he's the reason you need to work off fifteen hundred more calories. Don't touch the cake. Don't think about the cake.

Then he smiled again, and a dribble of sweat dripped down onto his abs, and my mouth popped open. What were we talking about?

"Let's meet up this weekend. Chase is having a party off campus, but maybe you can come over and we can work on it?" Chance asked, for what I assumed the second time, his eyebrow raised in questioning.

I bit my lip and nodded my head yes. I was going to have

major whiplash after today's meeting. I knew there was no way I could handle going over to Chases house, apartment or whatever, to study. I would have to cancel.

"'Kay. Talk then." Chance dismissed me and finished picking up his books and papers off the ground. I gave Chase one more once over and then walked away, wondering what the fuck it was I was doing. I had no reason to be lusting after someone like him. He was as far from the safe zone as it got. His demeanor alone caused my heartbeat to go into overdrive, my body to feel alive like no one else ever had. I knew better than to associate myself with him, to put myself in danger like that. For God's sake, my father was an FBI Agent if he heard half the shit I did away from home, he would be going to jail.

As I crossed the campus, my phone started to ring. "Fuck." I huffed, struggling to pull the slim device from the pocket of my shorts. Taylor's name showed across the screen, and excitement filled me as I pressed the answer key.

"I'm so excited to see you!" she squealed into the phone. Taylor was far more excited than I was. This was her first year of college, a time where growing was something she would truly experience. I was glad I would be that one friend there for her when she needed it most.

"I'm pretty sure I'm way more excited. I have to start packing up my stuff at the dorm this week," I confessed. I hated packing, moving, and anything that involved moving was something I was against.

"Poor thing. I did find a condo for rent. I'm going to call the number on Craigslist on Monday. I just wanted you to know I did find something to rent, hopefully. It's close to campus, and they're offering the apartment in the basement. Two bedrooms, one bathroom with a full kitchen." A smile formed on my face as I crossed the grass to my dorm room. I slid my key into the door, gaining access into the building.

"You've sure done your research. That sounds amazing,

the only issue is price." I hated to be the bearer of bad news, but I wanted to be realistic.

"They only want eight hundred a month." She sounded just as shocked as I felt. So much so, I almost tripped walking up the stairs.

"Well, shit. Then it's a given, as long as everything checks out and they aren't some serial killers—then, of course, we'll take it." My voice bounced off the empty hall as I jogged up another flight of stairs, keeping my eyes focused on every step.

"Yes, you bet your ass we will. I have to go, though." I could hear her moving around her bedroom.

"Okay…" I said, saddened our conversation had to end so soon. It had been three horrible, long years we had been separated. Now, we would finally be together doing what college kids did all across the country.

"Sorry, Dad wants to take me out to dinner. I'll text you when I get home." I said 'K' and she hung up. I pulled my phone away from my face just as I made it to my room. 208. I sighed into the air. There was no one here, no one to talk to, and no one to do anything with. I realized the highlight of my day had already come and gone as I threw myself onto my bed. Now I was free to do nothing the rest of the afternoon.

Sigh. College.

Acknowledgements

EVERY TIME I have to write this part of a book, I clam up. Not because I can't do it, but because I worry I'll forget something or someone. Therefore, right here, right now, I want to thank anyone who has picked up one of my books—either this series or another, it doesn't matter. Just thank you. To the many bloggers, authors, and street members who have helped me create and end an epic series in the last six months. You all are a true inspiration to me and my reason to keep writing. You keep being you, and I'll keep writing.

BETA TEAM: I love you ladies so much. Over the last year, you truly have become a part of my extended family. You have brought so much joy to my life, and nothing can or will ever take that away.

ROBIN: Thank you for the conversations about wine, and the fact that you help me become a better author with every "picky" word from your mouth. ;)

MEDIA TEAM: Thank you so flocking much. Without you lovely ladies, I would be nowhere, my books wouldn't reach anyone, and I would be on a little island alone.

TO LEE: Never give up on that dream of becoming an author. xoxo

BRIE: Even when you're a whore face, I love you. Thank you for making me a better author with every book I publish. You make me believe in myself like I never have before.

JENN, TASHA: You both supported me when I

needed you most. Thank you so much for being the best of friends.

MARY: I'm seriously a bad friend. Thank you for still being here through all this. MWAH!!!

HUBS: Are you even going to read this? ;) Love you!

BELLA: If you're reading this, you better be 18… I'm watching you.

About J. L. Beck

J.L. BECK IS THE Best Selling Author of A Kingpin Love Affair Series and The Bittersweet Series. She plays mother and wife by day and writer extraordinaire by night. When she's not writing, reading, or doodling, you can find her watching The Vampire Diaries and The 100. She currently resides in the tiny town of Elroy in the state of Wisconsin with her husband of seven years and their three-year-old hellion.

Stalk her — you know you want to:

FACEBOOK: https://www.facebook.com/Jo.L.Beck?ref=hl
TWITTER: https://twitter.com/AuthorJLBeck
GOODREADS: https://www.goodreads.com/user/show/23673426-j-l-beck
SIGN UP FOR HER NEWSLETTER: http://eepurl.com/2aydr